"You and Fay. You were just a few days old when this picture was taken."

The starch seemed to go out of Ariadne's knees. She sank back against the side of the desk. She couldn't believe she had a twin she'd never known about.

Clay settled himself beside her and slipped one arm around her shoulders. "Cry if you want to."

"No. I'm past that."

"If you'd like to talk, I'm a good listener."

"There's no question now," Ariadne admitted with a deep sigh. "But I don't…I just can't…"

Clay stood slowly and pulled her to her feet beside him. Desire coursed through him in a wave as thick and hot as a lava flow. He recognized the answering heat in Ariadne's eyes before they drifted slowly closed.

Clay caught himself a millisecond before he gave in to the urge to find out if her lips were as soft as they looked….

Dear Reader,

March is a month of surprises and a time when we wait breathlessly for the first hints of spring. A young man's fancy is beginning to turn to love...but then, in each Special Edition novel, thoughts of love are everywhere! And March has a whole bouquet of love stories for you!

I'm so pleased to announce that *Waiting for Nick* by Nora Roberts is coming your way this month. This heartwarming story features Freddie finally getting her man...the man she's been waiting for all of her life. Revisit the Stanislaskis in this wonderful addition to Nora Roberts's bestselling series, THOSE WILD UKRAINIANS.

If handsome rogues quicken your pulse, then don't miss *Ashley's Rebel* by Sherryl Woods. This irresistible new tale is the second installment of her new series, THE BRIDAL PATH. And Diana Whitney concludes her PARENTHOOD series this month—with *A Hero's Child*, an emotionally stirring story of lovers reunited in a most surprising way.

Three veteran authors return this month with wonderful new romances. Celeste Hamilton's *Marry Me in Amarillo* will warm your heart, and Carole Halston dazzles her readers once again with *The Wrong Man...The Right Time*. Kaitlyn Gorton's newest, *Separated Sisters*, showcases this talented writer's gift of portraying deep emotion with the joy of lasting love.

I hope that you enjoy this book, and each and every story to come!

Sincerely,

Tara Gavin,

Senior Editor

Please address questions and book requests to:
Silhouette Reader Service
U.S.: 3010 Walden Ave., P.O. Box 1325, Buffalo, NY 14269
Canadian: P.O. Box 609, Fort Erie, Ont. L2A 5X3

KAITLYN GORTON

SEPARATED SISTERS

SPECIAL EDITION®

Published by Silhouette Books
America's Publisher of Contemporary Romance

Clay and Ari's story wouldn't have existed without the input, encouragement
and unfailingly honest critiques provided by
"The Group": Nancy Dorr, Lynn Manley, Kelly McClymer,
Yvonne Murphy and Trudy Zothner. As a critique group, a support group
and, on occasion, a therapy group, they can't be beat.
Thanks, guys. This book is for the five of you and for my long-distance
critique partner, Mary Anne Frounfelker.

Acknowledgments
David M. Sanders, Attorney-at-Law, for information on
the Maine State bar exam.

SILHOUETTE BOOKS

ISBN 0-373-24092-9

SEPARATED SISTERS

Books by Kaitlyn Gorton

Silhouette Special Edition

Hearth, Home and Hope #942
Separated Sisters #1092

Silhouette Intimate Moments

Cloud Castles #307

KAITLYN GORTON

is a former librarian and teacher who lives in rural Maine with her husband and two cats. She is the author of four books for young readers, a study of sixteenth-century women and several historical romances under the name Kathy Lynn Emerson. She occasionally attempts cross-country skiing and owns a set of snowshoes, and she once built a spectacular snow fort, but most of the time, when she's not writing romances, she's curled up by the fireside and reading them rather than out there playing in the snow.

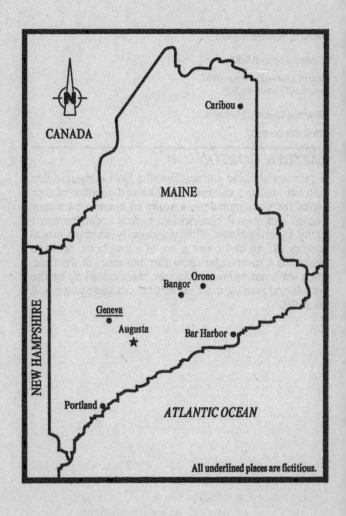

Caribou ●

CANADA

MAINE

Orono ●
Bangor ●

Geneva
●
Augusta
★

Bar Harbor ●

NEW HAMPSHIRE

Portland ●

ATLANTIC OCEAN

All underlined places are fictitious.

CHAPTER SEVEN

Chapter One

Clay Franklin stared at the slender, dark-haired woman seated on a high stool behind an antique cash register. He couldn't help himself. Even though he'd been prepared for her resemblance to her twin, it unnerved him. What bothered him even more was the jolt of sexual awareness he felt as he took a good, long look at Ariadne Palmer. *That* certainly never happened with Fay.

Both women had inherited the classic Grecian features of their great-grandmother, but Ariadne emphasized the sculpted lines by pulling the mass of sable curls away from her face and confining them in a practical coil at the nape of her neck. The style should have suggested a schoolmarm's bun, but the image forming in Clay's mind was far removed from the prim and proper. He wondered what it would feel like to release those soft tendrils, to let all that lustrous hair cascade down in enticing, sensual waves.

Clay frowned. He'd seen Fay with her hair loose more times than he could count, until she'd finally gotten tired of fussing with it and had it cut into a short bob. The sight had never made the least impression on his libido, not even when he was a horny eighteen-year-old and the two of them were all alone at the beach. He had, at most, a sort of brotherly affection for Fay Allandale.

What was so different about Fay's twin, a twin whose existence they hadn't even suspected until two months ago? Clay's mouth kicked up at the corner for a moment in wry, self-deprecating humor. How often had he wished he *could* generate some romantic interest in his childhood friend? A marriage between them would have pleased their matchmaking relatives enormously, but the spark simply hadn't been there. Their relationship was strictly platonic and had been from the time they'd first been introduced to each other. She'd just turned eight and he'd been nine and a half.

With an effort, Clay shifted his attention from Ariadne Palmer to her place of business. There were old books everywhere, but the atmosphere was more of a turn-of-the-century library than a secondhand bookstore. Along the back wall, behind the counter where Ariadne sat, shelves rose to a height of at least ten feet, the upper levels accessible only with the help of a tall, sliding ladder. Above that there was a narrow balcony that ran around three sides of the central room of the shop. Beneath the balcony on his right, Clay saw what appeared to be a converted sunporch, a large, square room with French doors.

Clay noted with approval that the most valuable

stock was kept in locked, glass-front display cases. Nearby, well-cared-for leather spines gleamed on shelves that held more run-of-the-mill nineteenth-century works. A faint aroma of lemon-scented furniture polish assaulted Clay's nostrils as he moved deeper into the shop.

Ariadne and her partner specialized in antiquarian books, but several sections of the store were devoted to newer hardcover titles, particularly mystery fiction and biography.

The whisper of a wool skirt against the silk slip beneath drew Clay's gaze back to Ariadne Palmer. For the second time that morning he felt desire slam into him. She'd looked up from her paperwork and suddenly he was drowning in the biggest brown eyes he'd ever seen.

They're just like Fay's eyes, he tried to tell himself. But he knew they weren't. Fay's eyes had never regarded him with so much purely feminine interest.

Clay was no stranger to admiring glances from women. He'd had the good fortune to inherit his mother's wholesome appearance, including wavy blond hair and hazel eyes and skin that looked as if it had a healthy tan even in midwinter. A successful career kept him in expensive but conservative business suits tailored to be comfortable. It was pure serendipity that the style also did justice to his father's genetic contribution, a broad-shouldered, naturally athletic build.

"Good morning," Ariadne said. "Isn't it a lovely day for early March?" Her voice was a pleasant contralto, much like Fay's, but with a faint huskiness that Clay found both charming and unique.

"Spring thaw," he replied. Which was why the door had been open and why he'd been able to study her for a few precious moments before she realized he was there. Yesterday, when the entire state of Maine had still been in a deep freeze, chimes would have announced him the moment he entered the bookstore.

As Ariadne slid off the stool and came around the counter toward him, a whiff of perfume preceded her—just a faint, sweet fragrance, but enough to trigger a brief vision of a field full of wildflowers and Ariadne in a gauzy dress.

Reining in the sudden flight of fancy, Clay stared hard at the woman approaching him, taking in clothes that were casual and inexpensive but very flattering. Her long, plaid skirt and a loose, rose-colored sweater emphasized a tall, willowy figure.

Slenderness had never seemed so appealing.

"Not spring thaw, yet, I'm afraid," she said in answer to his casual comment about the weather. "This is what we call false spring. Unfortunately, it never lasts more than a day or two."

False spring. The term seemed appropriate. Given the details Clay knew about Ariadne Palmer's past, she wasn't what she appeared to be, either. The air of openness and innocence that seemed to surround her didn't mean a thing, except that he'd do well to remember the reason he was here.

"We have some stock that's not on the shelves," she said. "If there's something in particular you're after, I can check in the storeroom for it."

When she moved near enough to touch, Clay automatically produced one of his business cards and handed it over. "I came here to find you, Ms. Palmer."

Frowning, Ariadne retreated a few steps to read the card. Her dark eyes were wary when she glanced his way again, but she kept her tone of voice polite. "You're a long way from Hartford, Mr. Franklin."

Clay smiled a bit grimly. He'd expected her to be impressed, but it appeared she'd never heard of the prestigious law firm to which he belonged. Perhaps that was just as well. It would be better if she didn't know quite yet that an Allandale could afford to hire the best.

"How can I help you, Mr. Franklin?" She pointedly put the wide, polished surface of the oak counter between them.

The outcome of this meeting had seemed straightforward, if not precisely simple, when he had agreed to follow up on the information gathered by a private investigator Fay had hired to find her long-lost twin. If Duncan's report was accurate then Ariadne had no idea that she had a sister. She knew nothing, either, of the existence of her maternal grandparents. She'd grown up believing that her paternal grandfather, Edward Palmer, was her only living relative.

It was Clay's first job to break the news.

He hesitated, momentarily uncertain how to begin. A blunt statement of the facts seemed best. "I've been sent here by your grandparents to—"

"My grandparents are dead." Her hand went to the gold locket she wore. She seemed to take comfort from the feel of its delicately engraved surface.

Warning himself not to sympathize with her, Clay's manner became formal. "Let me explain, Ms. Palmer. I do realize that your paternal grandfather died six months ago. You have my condolences. But your maternal grandparents are still alive. After your mother's recent death your—"

The liquid brown eyes darkened still more in irritation. "You're mistaking me for someone else, Mr. Franklin. My mother died when I was three years old."

So that's what she'd been told. Duncan hadn't been able to find out. Clay's voice gentled fractionally. "I know this must come as a shock to you, Ms. Palmer, but I'm telling you the truth. There is no mistake. Aside from everything else, the way you look is undeniable proof."

"I think you should leave now." In an unspoken threat, she reached for the telephone on the counter, prepared to quick-dial for help if he made any untoward moves.

Clay abruptly realized that he was handling this situation very badly. His normally rational mind must have short-circuited if he was allowing a woman's physical appearance to throw him off his stride. He prided himself on being able to remain unaffected by sexual attraction. Barbara had taught him that bitter lesson. He was almost glad she had. These days he knew better than to let desire interfere with common sense.

Deciding that it must be Ariadne's uncanny resemblance to Fay that was the problem, he fumbled in his breast pocket for a recent snapshot of Ariadne's twin. He placed it on the countertop between them. "Take a look at this, Ms. Palmer."

In the picture, Fay's short haircut wasn't immediately apparent because she was wearing a jacket with the collar turned up. Anyone glancing at it quickly would think that the woman in front of him now was its subject.

Ariadne kept one hand on the phone, using the fingers that had been nervously toying with her locket to pick up the snapshot. She stared at it for a long moment, frowning, then looked directly at Clay. Her expression contained equal parts of puzzlement and suspicion.

"I don't understand. I never posed for this shot. I don't even recognize the place where this picture was taken."

"That's because the woman in the photograph isn't you, Ms. Palmer. She's your sister, Fay. Your twin sister."

"Don't be absurd. I don't have a sister." Ariadne tried to hand the photo back to him but Clay refused to take it.

"On the contrary, you not only have a sister, you also have grandparents, and they are all interested in meeting you."

Ariadne reached across the counter and stuffed the offending picture back into the breast pocket of his jacket. "Please go away, Mr. Franklin. I don't know what you're trying to sell, but I'm not buying."

That she didn't believe him momentarily stymied Clay. He'd been certain the photograph would convince her. Never having considered the possibility that she might think he was lying, he reacted impulsively. "What's your birth date?"

"Is that a variant of 'What's your sign?' Please, Mr. Franklin! At least the line about a twin had the benefit of being a bit original."

Clay's astonishment grew. Now she was trying to humor him, obviously hoping he'd leave peacefully. Couldn't she see that he had no reason to make up such a story? After all, she was the one who stood to gain. He watched her face closely as he rattled off a date he knew as well as he knew his own birthday. This time, however, not even Ariadne's eyes gave anything away.

"You could have gotten that information in quite a number of places, Mr. Franklin," she said stiffly. "Some of them are even legal."

"And where would I have found another woman with both your face and your birth date?" He leaned closer. "This goes a little beyond coincidence, don't you think?"

"I think that you'd better—"

Hoping to provoke a reaction, he cut her off. "Haven't you ever wondered what happened to your parents?"

The dark eyes flashed again, then went blank as Ariadne withdrew both physically and emotionally. Her voice sounded curiously flat. "I know exactly what happened to them. They died in a car crash."

"Is that what your grandfather told you?"

"Yes." The word was clipped. Both hands curled into fists at her sides.

"Do you remember your parents at all?"

"I was three. How could I?" Her voice had dropped to below freezing and was getting colder by the second.

Clay forced himself to keep goading her even though she seemed to be sincere. Duncan's investigation had indicated that she had no knowledge of her mother's family. On the other hand, it had also suggested that Ariadne Palmer had a mercenary streak at least as wide as the Maine Turnpike.

Her inexpensive clothing, the absence of any jewelry but the locket, the lack of calculation in her reaction to his claims...all these factors argued for discounting the charges made against her. Until Clay remembered that she was Mark Palmer's daughter. And Mark Palmer had been, among other things, a scoundrel who'd demanded a cash settlement to divorce his wife.

Clay intended to keep pushing Ariadne until he could be certain just what kind of person she was. That was, after all, his second purpose in coming here. He rationalized that confronting her didn't harm anyone. He was just testing her reactions. It was a legitimate way of looking out for Fay's best interests, as her lawyer and as her friend.

"All you have," he said derisively, "is Edward Palmer's word as to what happened to them."

One of her clenched fists slammed down on the highly polished oak countertop between them. Heat replaced her chill and Ariadne's voice crackled with emotional flames. "How dare you!"

"Ms. Palmer—"

"My grandfather would *never* lie to me." Rounding the counter she advanced on him, clearly intending to throw him out if he didn't leave voluntarily.

Clay prudently retreated, impressed by the depth of her confidence in her late grandfather. The fact that the man *had* lied was hardly relevant at the moment. As he backed away, Clay kept his eyes on her face, mildly amused—in spite of the circumstances—to discover that there was truth in the old cliché. Some women *were* beautiful when they were angry. Ariadne Palmer was one of them.

"Search your memory, Ms. Palmer," he said when he reached the exit. "Look at your own recollections, not just those things you were told as a child. When you decide you're ready to talk with me, you can find me at Trudy's Bed and Breakfast on Zothner Street."

He didn't bother to add that if he didn't hear from her soon he'd be back. If she was as smart as her sister, she'd figure that out on her own.

As soon as the intruder was safely out of her shop, Ariadne collapsed into a high-backed, well-upholstered wing chair. She felt confused and angry...and just a bit frightened.

What he'd said couldn't be true.

Could it?

No, of course not. Family loyalty quickly reasserted itself. Her grandfather had been a kind, loving, honest man. He'd never have deceived her the way this Connecticut lawyer insinuated that he had.

Still, there had to be some reason why Clayton Franklin would come here with such a preposterous story. She frowned. In spite of her conviction that he was wrong, she wasn't certain he was lying. He had struck her as a man who believed what he was saying. He hadn't brought out that picture with the air of a magician conjuring up a trick, but rather with the calm assurance of an advocate presenting irrefutable proof of his claim.

Closing her eyes for a moment, she took a deep breath.

Was it possible? Eyes still closed, Ariadne envisioned the photograph. It might have been convincing evidence a few decades ago, but everyone nowadays knew how easy it was to fake that sort of thing. The scandal magazines made their fortunes by it.

Reality check. Open eyes. Scan surroundings. Ariadne obeyed her own silent orders and was relieved to discover that nothing in the shop had changed. That very solid fact had a calming effect.

The central room of the bookstore had originally been the private library of the Chatsworth house. It still retained much of that atmosphere, especially in the spiral staircase to the balcony and the number of comfortable chairs and small, oak tables that were liberally scattered among the stacks for the convenience of browsers. After Ariadne's longtime friend and current business partner, Laurie Chatsworth, had arranged for them to buy the place from her retiring parents at a bargain price, they'd knocked down walls on two sides to add the formal dining room and the sunroom to their business premises. While Laurie made her home in the remainder of the Victorian mansion, Ariadne and her four-year-old daughter lived in the apartment above the garage.

This is reality, Ariadne assured herself. And she liked the life she'd built for herself and Shanna. She had a healthy, happy child, a job she liked and no emotional complications. They might not have a lot of money, but they got by. She wanted to keep things just as they were, for Shanna's sake as well as for her own.

Clayton Franklin did not fit into the picture. He was a disruptive influence. But why would he make up a story about a twin? Was he running some kind of con game? Ariadne couldn't think what he hoped to gain. The most valuable book in the store was only worth a few hundred dollars. There wasn't a Gutenberg Bible in the lot.

Whatever he wanted, Ariadne resolved to put a stop to his scheme. She'd simply refuse to have anything more to do with him. Her mind made up, she turned her attention to the accounts she'd been working on earlier.

Ten minutes later she was staring off into space, remembering things she didn't really want to think about at all, when Laurie opened the hidden door on the balcony. The door looked like just another bookcase when it was closed, but actually connected the shop to Laurie's second-floor office. "Ari?"

Startled, Ariadne sucked in a sharp breath.

"What's wrong?" Laurie demanded. She descended to the main salesroom at a snail's pace, since it was against her principles to rush anywhere, but there was no mistaking her avid interest in her friend's odd behavior.

"Nothing," Ariadne said hastily. "I just didn't hear you come in."

Laurie's response was a snort of disbelief. Ariadne braced herself. Her friend had the curiosity of a cat and the tenacity of a bulldog. When she wanted answers, she generally got them.

"You're not depressed because business is off, are you?" Laurie gestured toward the ledgers piled on the counter. "It's the time of year. Things will pick up as soon as mud-season is over. And the mail-order department's doing just fine."

"I'm not depressed at all. Honest." Ariadne pasted on a smile and hoped for the best.

Behind big, round glasses, Laurie's nearsighted blue eyes gave Ariadne the disconcerting impression that she could see right through her. Laurie's words confirmed that it would do Ariadne no good to try and dissemble. "You may as well confess, Ari. You know you'll end up telling me eventually. What is it that's bugging you?"

"You've known me too long," Ariadne grumbled.

She'd first met Laurie in college and there were few secrets they did not share. Resigned, she gave her friend an edited account of the handsome lawyer's visit. His claims seemed even more preposterous to her when she repeated them aloud. She expected Laurie to laugh, and felt uneasy when she did not.

"What if he's telling the truth?" Laurie asked.

"Don't be absurd."

"Well, you don't know anything about your mother's parents, do you? You don't know when they died, or where they're buried."

"No. I don't. But I'm sure Gramps would have told me if they were still alive."

Frowning, Ariadne tried to remember if Gramps had ever said anything at all about her other grandparents. He hadn't liked to talk about the tragedy that had left her an orphan. To keep from making him sad, she'd learned at an early age to avoid the entire subject of family.

One of these days, Shanna would be asking the same sort of questions Ariadne had at her age. Ariadne had already thought out what she'd say to explain why she and Shanna's father hadn't married and why Brad never came to see his daughter, even though he lived only a few miles away. Ariadne didn't need a host of new relations clouding the issue, especially if acknowledging their existence meant she'd have to agree that Gramps had deceived her.

It all came back to that, and she wouldn't believe he'd deliberately lie. Yes, he'd sometimes been evasive, but she clung to the conviction that he'd always told the truth. She remembered one discussion they'd had, only a few months before he died. She'd been wondering if she should lie to Shanna about the circumstances of her birth. Gramps had insisted that it was always better to be honest.

"It's possible you do have family," Laurie said.

Abandoning her high stool, Ariadne began to pace.

"This business about a twin is just plain nonsense. Identical twins are supposed to have some kind of special bond. Wouldn't I have *known* if I had a twin sister?"

Laurie's eyes were bright behind the glasses. Tucking short wisps of unruly, sand-colored hair behind her ears, she leaned her elbows on the counter and propped her chin on her fists. "Not if you went through some kind of trauma when you were separated. Something that made you blank out all your early memories. How did the lawyer explain your being brought up apart?"

"He didn't." Laurie's eyes widened, but before she could say a word, Ariadne made a slashing motion with one arm. "No. Don't even suggest it. I am not going to contact him and ask. I don't want to hear another word on the subject. The whole thing is just too unbelievable. I don't know why I'm even talking about it. Either Mr. Franklin is mistaken or he's lying to me for some reason I can't begin to comprehend. Either way, I don't want to see him again."

"Ari," Laurie said gently, "you can't just ignore this and hope it goes away. You saw a photograph of a woman who looks just like you. Who is she if she's not your twin?"

"Everyone has a look-alike somewhere. That's all it is." Ariadne stopped pacing, momentarily lost in thought. That would explain it, wouldn't it? "It's all a mistake, Laurie. Coincidence. Or a trick of some kind. The only possible way for me to deal with it is to put him and his crazy story out of my mind right this minute."

The fortuitous arrival of a customer helped Ariadne do just that, but only until she'd rung up the sale. As soon as she had time to brood, the image of Clayton

Franklin returned to haunt her. "Damn him," she muttered.

"Not so easy to forget, huh?" Laurie was trying not to look amused, and failing miserably.

A wry, answering smile on her lips, Ariadne shrugged. "It's probably just because I'd decided, in that brief moment before he made his ridiculous claim, that he was an attractive man and I wouldn't mind getting to know him better. That just goes to show how little first impressions are worth!"

It wasn't like her to be taken in, even briefly, by a set of broad shoulders and wavy blond hair. Not after her experience with Brad. But at least this time she'd caught on quickly.

"Never judge a book by its cover," Laurie murmured, managing to echo her friend's thoughts with uncanny precision. She stretched lazily and then held out a hand.

"What?"

"You said he gave you his business card. I want a look at it."

Ariadne produced the small white rectangle from her skirt pocket, feeling the embossing beneath her thumb as she handled it. Laurie glanced at the firm's name and address, then tapped the edge of the card against her chin.

"I wonder..."

"What?"

Instead of answering, Laurie picked up the phone and punched in the number on the card. "Yes," she said when someone answered at the other end. "I wonder if you can confirm that a Mr. Clayton Franklin works for your firm?" She listened a moment. "Perhaps you could tell me what the younger one looks like? I want to be certain we're talking about the same man."

Laurie repeated each bit of description, waiting for Ariadne's nod. "Yes, that's the man. And you say he's out of state at the moment?" While she continued to listen, Laurie put her hand over the mouthpiece and whispered, "There are two Clayton Franklins with the firm. Senior and Junior. Junior handles most of the firm's divorce and child-custody work and goes by Clay."

Clay. The nickname made him seem more human. Better to think of him in terms of his profession, she decided. Divorce lawyer? That brought an appropriately negative image to mind. Preoccupied, Ariadne briefly lost the thread of Laurie's phone conversation. She was puzzled when her friend began to describe a second man.

"He's about six feet tall, with dark hair and eyes and a rugged build," Laurie said. "He's got a small scar on his left cheek and he looks as if he's had his nose broken at least once. I believe he works for your firm but I didn't get his name."

Listening to the answer, Laurie's expression clouded. Whatever information was being provided by the person at the other end of the phone line, it was not what she wanted to hear. On a scratch pad in front of her, Laurie inscribed a name: Duncan Lords. Then she crossed out Lords and wrote in Lourdes. "Like the shrine in France?" she asked and smiled reluctantly at the answer she received. "No saint, huh? I'll just bet he isn't. Thanks." When she cradled the receiver she had a troubled look on her face.

"Who's Duncan Lourdes?"

Ariadne was fairly certain that Laurie's interest in

him wasn't personal. Her friend always claimed she wasn't the type to attract a husband and she went out of her way to make sure she didn't accidentally court male attention, concealing an abundantly female figure with long, loose, shapeless caftans and L.L. Bean jumpers. Most people, as she intended, assumed she was overweight and using the flowing garments to hide unsightly bulges.

"Apparently, Mr. Lourdes is a private investigator, but when he was in here he was calling himself Mr. London and pretending to be a rare-book collector. I'd still think he was, if he'd given me a real address, but it turned out to be a dud." Laurie ripped the top sheet off the notepad and crumpled it as if she'd like to do the same to the man whose name was written there. "He's 'frequently employed by Franklin, Manley, Murphy, Franklin and Teasdale,'" Laurie said, mimicking the voice in Hartford. "I thought I was crazy to ask, but for once one of my hunches was right on the money. I'm only sorry I didn't catch on sooner."

"Wait a minute," Ariadne interrupted. "Are you saying this guy was sent here to investigate me?" The very idea sparked her notoriously quick temper.

"I'm afraid so. A couple of weeks ago. You weren't here. Not that he asked for you."

"But something must have made you suspicious of him."

Laurie shrugged and looked bemused. "At the time he just seemed…memorable."

"Was he acting oddly?"

"Only in that he was being very charming." She made a face.

Ariadne's eyes widened. Laurie was taking this very personally. "He came on to you?"

"Drop it, okay? The point is that he asked a lot of questions and he gave me a phony address in case I found the book he claimed he was after."

"The nerve of the man." Ariadne almost wished Clay Franklin would come back, just so she could give him a piece of her mind.

"He seemed so interested in the business—how we got started. Said he was considering becoming a dealer himself. I didn't tell him much of anything, of course. Not about your personal life, or anything, but—"

Alarmed by the sudden silence, Ariadne took a step closer to her friend. "What?"

Laurie hesitated. The expression on her face had changed yet again, altering from mere chagrin to reflect a deeper distress. "Oh, boy. Ari, I'm afraid you aren't going to like this."

"Why doesn't that surprise me? Give, Laurie. How much worse can it be than what you've already told me?"

"I just remembered. Lourdes didn't just talk to me. It was one day when I was keeping an eye on Shanna for you. He asked her questions, too."

Ariadne's indignation escalated into a flare of impotent rage so strong that she had to cling to the counter until the first shock had passed. A simmering anger stayed with her even after she'd controlled that first primal urge to do violence to any man vile enough to involve an innocent child in his schemes. Only a small part of what she was feeling was directed toward Duncan Lourdes.

"How dare he?" Ariadne demanded, her voice harsh with suppressed fury. "How dare Clay Franklin send someone here to harass my daughter!"

Clay returned to the bookstore the next morning. He was surprised when he saw no immediate sign of Ariadne. Only ten minutes earlier, from the window of his room in the bed and breakfast, a room chosen specifically for its catercorner view of the Chatsworth house from across two backyards, he'd seen her return from taking her four-year-old to day care. She'd gone directly into the shop.

"Be with you in a sec," an unfamiliar voice called when the door chimes ceased their racket. False spring was already on its way out and the temperature outside was hovering around the freezing mark.

"No rush," Clay said, glancing toward the speaker. She was up on the ladder, dusting the volumes on the highest shelves. Laurie Chatsworth, Ariadne's partner. The woman looked like a throwback to the days of flower children, decked out in a flowing purple caftan and layers of beads. Her straight, baby-fine hair was full of static, creating a wild halo around her plain, unpainted face.

"Mr. Franklin, I presume?" Laurie's expression was smug as she descended and faced him.

"What gave me away? No, don't answer that. You got a description from your partner." He didn't imagine it had been a flattering one. "I told Ms. Palmer the truth, Ms. Chatsworth."

"Laurie."

"Laurie. I'm Clay. Perhaps you can help me convince your friend that I'm not here to cause trouble for her. On the contrary. Her grandfather—"

"My grandfather is dead." Ariadne stood on the balcony above, glowering at them. As she came down the stairs, the temperature in the room abruptly rose, and when she reached the bottom and spoke he felt scalded by her words.

"I want you out of my shop, Mr. Franklin," she

said. "I have no interest in talking to you, now or ever."

"We have business to discuss, Ms. Palmer."

Ariadne looked as if she wanted to throw the steaming contents of her coffee mug into his face. That she thought better of it clearly had more to do with the damage stray drops might do to the books than with any consideration for his safety.

"Wise choice," he murmured. "Fay actually did that to me once. With hot chocolate. I'd just as soon not repeat the experience." Hoping to pique her curiosity about Fay, he added, "Your sister rarely acts out of anger, but she can be impulsive. She wanted to take me down a peg or two for a rude remark I made about one of her friends. She was thirteen at the time."

"It isn't a *friend* I'm concerned about, Mr. Franklin. Your spy questioned my daughter."

If a glare could strike a man dead, Ariadne's would have been fatal, but Clay understood her vehemence now. The maternal urge to protect young was a powerful force and one he knew better than to trifle with. He chose his next words with care. "Your daughter happened to be here when Duncan stopped by. And as I understand it, she asked more questions than he did." Four-year-olds, or so he'd been told, were like that.

Taking a careful sip of her coffee, Ariadne contemplated Clay over the rim. He stared back, sympathetic in spite of their adversarial relationship and his suspicions about her character.

Whatever else she might be, Ariadne Palmer was also an indignant, beautiful woman frustrated by circumstances beyond her control.

Chapter Two

A few minutes later, Ariadne waved Clay Franklin into the chair next to the computer in Laurie's office and seated herself behind the desk. "Talk," she ordered bluntly. "Tell me how I can have an identical twin sister and know nothing about it. Explain why you think my grandfather never mentioned her."

"You and your sister were separated when your parents divorced. You were less than a year old at the time."

Startled, she wanted to deny it, but before she could say a word he fixed her with a level gaze that dared her to disbelieve him.

"Your parents met in college," he explained. "They eloped when your mother found out she was pregnant. She gave birth to twins six months later. Shortly after that, your parents split up and agreed to have no further contact with each other, each keeping one twin, which meant that you and Fay were kept apart, too.''

With a small sound of distress, Ariadne sprang to her feet. "I won't listen to any more of your lies!"

She put her hands over her ears and would have fled if he hadn't been quick enough to stop her. He wrapped one hand around each of her wrists and pulled her arms down. He was surprisingly strong, fully capable of keeping her in his grip and forcing her to listen.

"Truth. All of it."

"No. My parents were never divorced. They lived here in Maine and they loved each other until the day they died. Together."

"I'm sorry, but that's not the way it happened. Your mother never even visited Maine. And she was still alive until very recently. As for your father—"

"You've made a mistake," she insisted. "I know that some men do father children and don't care anything about being part of their lives, but not *my* father."

"You've already admitted you don't remember him. Think, Ariadne. After he died, your grandfather might have been afraid to tell anyone the truth. Your father had legal custody of you, but after his death you should have been returned to your mother. Your grandfather was breaking the law by keeping you."

"That is completely absurd! If you think I'll let you get away with slandering my father and my grandfather, you—"

The lawyer talked right over her sputtered protests, apparently determined to tell her the rest of the story, even if he had to immobilize her in order to do so. "Your sister was brought up by your maternal grandparents, George and Lila Allandale. They knew Fay had a twin, but it wasn't until your mother died earlier this year that Fay found out. As soon as she recovered from the shock she hired Duncan Lourdes to find you.''

"I don't believe a word of this.'' Ariadne continued her futile struggle to free herself.

"You'll have to eventually.'' Held as she was, face-to-face with him, she could see the sincerity in his eyes...and something more. Without warning, he released her and resumed his seat.

Rubbing her wrists, Ariadne subsided into her own chair. All at once she felt too weary to fight him anymore. The stuffing had gone out of her, along with her anger. "What proof do you have?''

"Birth certificates, and a few old photographs.''

"Where are these pictures now? Why didn't you show them to me yesterday?''

"Because they wouldn't prove anything to you unless you had something to compare them to. *Do* you have any photographs of your mother?''

"No,'' she admitted reluctantly. That had bothered her a great deal when she was growing up, but she'd never really questioned her grandfather's explanation of the lack. Her mother had been camera-shy, Gramps had said.

The lawyer was silent, giving her time to think over all he'd said. She searched his story for flaws and had to admit that it sounded annoyingly plausible.

"It could have been some other Mark Palmer who fathered twins,'' she said in an irritated voice. Realizing even as she made the suggestion that it sounded absurd, she went on the offensive. "What took you so long to find me? And why did Fay, who claims to be my twin, send her lawyer here instead of contacting me directly?''

Neither his expressionless face nor his carefully

bland voice gave anything away. "It's a big country. And you weren't exactly separated yesterday. Your grandparents didn't know much about their daughter's husband. They hadn't approved of the marriage. You were finally located through the address on your father's college records."

All that sounded reasonable enough...except for the part that implied Gramps had been a liar. She bristled at the very thought. "Why am I even arguing about this? I am not anyone's missing twin. There's simply been a mix-up. You've got the wrong person."

"Do you know who you were named after, Ariadne?"

"Of course. Gramps was a big fan of Agatha Christie mysteries. One of her detectives is a woman named Ariadne Oliver."

"Your grandfather didn't name you. Your mother did. She had Greek ancestry and an interest in mythology. She named one of her daughters Ariadne and the other Phaedra."

Ariadne knew the legend, though she'd never liked it. In Greek mythology, Ariadne was the daughter of the king of Crete, the one who built the Labyrinth to imprison the Minotaur and demanded that human sacrifices be sent to him from Athens. Ariadne fell in love with one of them, Theseus, and helped him kill the Minotaur, only to have Theseus abandon her on an island on his way back to Athens. To add insult to injury, years later Theseus married Ariadne's sister, Phaedra.

"Your father was Mark Edward Palmer," Clay Franklin said in a surprisingly gentle voice.

"That's right, and—"

"Your mother was named Phyllis."

Ariadne shifted uneasily in her chair. "My mother's maiden name was Brown."

"Brown?"

"Brown," she repeated, but not as firmly as she would have liked. What if Clay Franklin *was* telling her the truth?

"And do *you* have a birth certificate?"

She glared at him, refusing to answer. She hadn't had a birth certificate because she'd been born at home and no one had thought to register the birth. That was what Gramps had told her when she'd needed one. He'd gone with her to the state's Office of Vital Statistics to remedy the situation by swearing he'd witnessed her birth. But when he'd been asked for her mother's name, to fill in on the form, he'd hesitated. After a moment he'd said it was Phyllis Brown. It had seemed to Ariadne, even then, that he was being evasive, but she hadn't called him on it. She'd trusted him.

The expression on Franklin's face was a combination of smug satisfaction and heartfelt sympathy. It provoked equally contradictory impulses in Ariadne. She wanted to slap him. At the same time she wanted to throw herself into his arms and be comforted.

Instead of doing either, she stared at her hands, which were now tightly clasped in her lap. She hated this. He was telling her that Gramps had lied to her all her life. Straightening her spine, she glared at him. Gramps had brought her up to be truthful. He *couldn't* have deceived her that way. And he'd *never* have kept a child separated from its mother.

"I don't believe a word you've said. If she's so convinced that I'm her missing twin, why did my alleged sister send you here to talk to me instead of coming in person?"

He looked uncomfortable when she repeated the same question she'd asked earlier, but this time he answered it. "Your grandparents asked her to be cautious."

"Why?"

"They're elderly, and a bit suspicious of anyone they don't know." He shrugged.

"That doesn't explain anything," she pointed out. "Why isn't this…Phaedra here with you?"

"Fay's a little…fragile right now. She and her husband are separated and contemplating divorce. I came not only because I'm her lawyer but also because I've been her friend since we were in grade school together."

"You're a divorce lawyer."

"I take it you don't think much of my profession." He sounded mildly amused.

Ariadne had no idea what to say next. It was a crazy story, one she should utterly reject, and yet he had succeeded in planting one small kernel of doubt in her mind. Could Gramps have deceived her? Had he been so afraid of losing custody of her that he'd lied to her all her life?

The possibility appalled her. Accepting it meant that he'd deliberately deprived her of the chance to know her mother. No! She wouldn't believe that. Her sense of betrayal at the very idea was too enormous. Gramps wouldn't have misled her about so much for so many years. Not if he'd been the kind of man she'd thought he was.

A little desperately, she clutched at the gold locket she always wore. It contained pictures of her grandfather and his wife, the paternal grandmother who had died the year after Ariadne was born. Why, the next

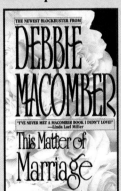

This Matter of Marriage

**delivers warmth, humor, romance—
a definite "feel-good" reading experience!**

❧ ❧ ❧

From Hallie McCarthy's Diary:

A new year generally starts out with me writing a few inspiring lines about how I'm going to lose five pounds—let's be honest, it's ten—and pay off all my credit cards, and other high expections like that. It's the same every January. But *this* year's going to be different.

Oh, I still want to lose those extra pounds, more than ever, but for a different reason.

I want a husband. And eventually a family.

And that means I need a plan. Being a goal-oriented person, I start by identifying what I'm after (MARRIAGE!) and then I work out a logical procedure for getting it. Which, in this case, includes *looking good*. (Not that I look bad now, if I do say so myself. But I'm talking *really* good. Are you listening, thighs?) Because, as I've learned in advertising, *packaging counts*.

So, last week I made *the* decision: *Marriage!*

❧ ❧ ❧

And be sure to look for Debbie's October 1997 title, THREE BRIDES, NO GROOM...three brand-new stories of three friends who discover that Mr. Right has turned into Mr. Wrong...but that doesn't stop them from finding true love—and marriage.

thing she knew, Clay Franklin would be telling her that
Grandma Palmer was just a figment of her imagination.
He seemed that intent on disproving every single thing
she'd ever believed about herself and her family.

"I think you should leave now," Ariadne told the
lawyer.

He didn't argue, apparently satisfied that he'd done
enough damage for one morning. Ariadne stared at his
broad back, watching him walk away with an easy
stride until he was out of sight. All the while she was
beset by the disquieting certainty that she had not seen
the last of Clayton Franklin.

Clay's first priority after he left the bookstore was
to find a phone and call Ariadne's twin sister.

"Finally!" she greeted him. "What's going on
there? I expected to hear from you yesterday. Did you
meet her?"

Had he ever. "Yes, I met her."

"And?"

"So far she's reluctant to believe a single word of
the story I told her."

"Well, who wouldn't be? What is she like?"

"She looks just like you but she has more of a temper."

"Is that good or bad? Never mind. I don't want to
know." Fay's nervous laughter broke Clay's heart. The
troubles in her marriage had been a blow to her self-
confidence. "When can I meet her?"

"It may be a while yet. Things here are more…
complicated than I anticipated."

"How so?"

Clay hesitated, his hand gripping the phone with
greater force than he needed. He'd always found Fay's

voice pleasant. Why was he suddenly so aware of the fact that it lacked that sensual huskiness Ariadne's possessed?

"Clay? Are you still there?"

"Yeah. Sorry. And I apologize for not calling sooner. Is everything okay? No trouble with Gary?"

While Fay assured him that her estranged husband was not a problem and filled him in on their last session with the marriage counselor Clay had recommended, Clay's mind began to wander again, this time back to the previous evening. He'd gone out intending to phone Fay from the privacy of a pay phone. Somehow, he'd ended up standing in front of the Chatsworth mansion instead, staring up at the windows above the garage. By the time the lights winked out and he remembered why he'd left the bed and breakfast in the first place, he realized it was after ten. He'd told himself it was too late at night to disturb Fay, but the truth was that he'd been reluctant just then to talk to her, or anyone else, about Ariadne.

"Clay? When are you coming back to Connecticut?"

"I need to stay on top of things here." He winced at his word choice and was glad Fay couldn't know what he was thinking. "I want to continue to handle this case in person."

"Why?"

"I'm not sure yet what to make of her."

"If it's that difficult to judge her character, maybe I should be there."

"You promised your grandfather you'd wait."

Fay sighed deeply. "I know Poppa means well, but I wish he wouldn't be quite so overprotective. It's not like I'm still a child."

Fay's grandfather, George Allandale, was convinced that Ariadne would take after her father, who had been more interested in a quick buck than he'd ever been in Phyllis Allandale. George had badgered Fay, trying to get her to drop the idea entirely of meeting her twin. In the end they'd compromised and agreed to have Clay make the first contact. George had set one oth r condition. Clay was to keep secret from Ariadne the fact that the Allandales were wealthy.

"This is absurd," Fay continued. "Why should I have to put off meeting my sister until Poppa takes a look at her? She's not really a gold digger, is she?"

"It's too soon to tell." It didn't look like it, but Clay had been deceived by a pretty face once before. He was taking no chances.

"Consider the source," Fay reminded him. She was talking about Mrs. Emmaline Comfort, Shanna's paternal grandmother, who had given Duncan Lourdes a lurid account of the college romance between Ariadne and her son Brad and claimed Ariadne had tried to trap him into marriage by getting pregnant.

"Brad Comfort confirmed the details." Their interviews with Duncan, combined with details of Ariadne's partnership with Laurie Chatsworth, a partnership to which Laurie had contributed both her house and most of their capital, did make Ariadne look like a woman inclined to latch on to other people's assets and use them for her own ends.

"Is she after you yet?" Fay asked.

"What?"

"Well, if she's only interested in money, you're certainly a good catch. Is she throwing herself at you?"

"No." More to himself than to Fay, he added, "It

would make things easier if she did. Then maybe I could seduce the truth out of her."

"Clay!"

"Sorry. Just a thought." An intriguing one, too, although hardly his usual way of dealing with women.

"How much have you told her?" Fay asked.

"Only what we agreed to when you and I flew to Florida for that strategy session at your grandfather's winter home." Clay's free hand strayed to the back of his neck, trying to ease a sudden knot of tension. The fact that George was one of his firm's most important clients made it inevitable that what George wanted, George got.

Just because Clay didn't care for George Allandale's tactics, he reminded himself, didn't mean the old man was wrong about Ariadne. That was why he hadn't wasted time arguing. Besides, he'd learned as a child to accept George's word as law.

"Good," Fay said, surprising him.

"Good? I thought you were opposed to keeping secrets."

"I am. But part of me hopes she'll never have to know that our father took money to agree to the divorce."

"Right now she won't even accept the fact that there was a divorce. She was told that her parents were together when they died. That they loved each other until the end."

"I didn't think anyone believed in happily ever after anymore." Fay sounded wistful.

"She won't much longer. Not once she has proof that her grandfather made the whole thing up."

"Do you have any idea how cynical you sound?"

"Let's face it, Fay. I've seen too much evidence to the contrary to believe that any marriage can last."

Too late, he remembered she was trying to save hers. He could have bitten his tongue. It wasn't like him to be so tactless. But before he could apologize, Fay abruptly changed the subject.

"Is she a cute kid? Shanna?"

"I haven't met her yet," he admitted.

"Good grief, Clay. Stop fooling around. Don't you know that one of the best ways to judge character is to watch the way a person behaves around a child?"

"Hey, pumpkin! How was your day?" Ariadne planted an affectionate kiss in the cluster of light brown curls on top of Shanna's head.

"I had fun, Mommy." An impish smile was all it took to emphasize Shanna's elfin features. She had the look of a mischievous wood sprite as she added, "Mary Sue Pritchard peed in her pants."

"How lovely for her mother." Ignoring Laurie's sympathetic snort of laughter, Ariadne hurriedly finished up the few odds and ends of business that needed to be done before she could go home.

It hadn't been her most productive day. Ever since her meeting with Clay Franklin in Laurie's office that morning, she'd had a hard time concentrating on the bookstore.

For the next few hours, though, Ariadne knew her daughter would keep her too busy to dwell on the questions the Connecticut lawyer had raised. A detailed account of all of Shanna's adventures at day care took them across the dooryard and up the stairs to their apartment. As usual, the little girl complained about the required nap.

"Didn't you sleep?" Ariadne asked she unlocked her front door.

Shanna didn't answer, which meant she had and didn't want to admit it. Ariadne wisely dropped the subject. "What do you want to do while I fix supper?" she asked.

"Play-Doh."

There were worse choices. Shanna might have picked finger paints. Once divested of coats and hats and mittens, Ariadne settled her daughter at one end of the kitchen table and handed over two yellow canisters of aqua Play-Doh and a plastic bag full of holiday cookie cutters. Shanna liked to make snowmen and Christmas trees no matter what the season.

"All set?" Ariadne asked as she began to fill the remaining half of the table with the things she'd be needing to prepare and serve their evening meal. Space was at a premium in this kitchen. She made one pile of plates, silverware, glasses and napkins and next to them placed the oven mitts she'd use to take the broiled hamburgers out of the oven and the colander she'd need to drain the macaroni for the macaroni and cheese.

"All set?" she asked again.

"All set," Shanna echoed, happily preoccupied.

Satisfied, Ariadne turned her back on her daughter in order to chop raw vegetables on the cutting board next to the sink. She made the mistake of looking out the small window over it. Through the trees and back-yards she could just see the roof of the bed and break-fast where Clay Franklin had said he was staying.

Did she owe it to Shanna to make contact with this new family? If, indeed, they were her family.

Ariadne was aware that her daughter missed Bumpa,

her great-grandfather, terribly. And she knew it was good for a child to have a strong male influence in her life. Not just any man would do, though. She'd have insisted Brad spend time with his daughter if that were the case. No, it was far better to have no man at all than to admit a bad influence. She would have to be as cautious about this new family as she was with Brad's.

Now that Ariadne thought about it, the story Clay Franklin had told her of her parents' college romance had a few uncanny parallels with her own experience, except that in her case there had been no marriage before the split. She paused in the act of dumping a cup of uncooked macaroni into a pot of boiling water. Brad hadn't wanted anything to do with her after she'd told him she was pregnant with Shanna. He'd seen his daughter exactly once, when she was still a tiny baby, and only then because Laurie, who was Brad's cousin, had insisted.

The pasta plopped into the pot, splashing scalding water close to Ariadne's hand. Biting back an expletive, she seized a wooden spoon and gave the macaroni a quick stir, then prudently turned the heat down.

"Mommy, look," Shanna announced. "Worms."

Uncertain what to expect, Ariadne turned. Her daughter had appropriated the colander. Play-Doh now filled it halfway to the brim and when Shanna pushed down with the heel of her hand, thin aqua "worms" squiggled through each of the holes in the bottom.

Helpless to do otherwise, Ariadne began to laugh. "I guess a little Play-Doh flavor in the pasta never hurt anyone," she managed to say.

"That's gross, Mommy."

At the expression on Shanna's face, Ariadne laughed

harder, until tears streamed down her cheeks. She gave
Shanna a big hug. "Gross, huh? Then I guess you'll
just have to do a really good job washing the colander."

After they'd eaten and Shanna had helped wash all
the dishes, Ariadne and her daughter watched television together for an hour. Then Ariadne read Shanna a
story and tucked her into bed. She was tired herself,
but she knew she would not be able to sleep. There
was still too much on her mind.

She wished more than anything that she still had
Gramps to talk to. He'd always known what was best
to do.

Or had he?

To her dismay, Ariadne's faith in him was wavering.
All day long, she'd fought an insidious inclination to
believe Clay Franklin, especially if he could provide
proof that what he'd told her was true. Then her determination not to doubt her grandfather's veracity, not
even for a moment, would return. She told herself that
this was a test of her loyalty to the man who'd raised
her. Even when common sense had urged her to call
Franklin and demand more details, she'd fought the
impulse.

Ariadne had not allowed herself to think about Phaedra at all. She'd always wanted a sister but accepting
that she had one meant accepting everything she'd been
told. She wasn't ready to do that. Not by a long shot.

When she was sure Shanna was asleep, Ariadne began to pace. She felt trapped in the small apartment. It
was pleasant enough. What she and Laurie now used
as a garage had originally been a carriage house, and
the former servants' quarters above it were quite com-

fortable. But tonight it felt like a prison, and she was locked in with her unwelcome speculations.

She stopped in front of her grandfather's desk, one of the few pieces of his furniture that she'd kept after he died. Edward Palmer's personal papers still filled its drawers and pigeonholes.

If there was proof anywhere that Clay Franklin was wrong, she realized, it was here. She'd been through the contents once, of course, but she hadn't had the heart to look closely at everything. There might be something she'd missed, some evidence that what Gramps had always told her *was* the truth.

The moment she opened the drop-leaf front, she was overwhelmed by nostalgia…and by the distinctive scent of spearmint chewing gum. Gramps had been addicted to the stuff. There had always been loose sticks of it in the pigeonholes. There still were.

She almost gave up then. Only the thought of Clay Franklin and his outrageous claims kept her going. This was the one thing she could think of to do to prove him wrong. Inhaling a deep, steadying breath, she opened the first small drawer.

Fifteen minutes later she'd examined everything, from World War II medals and letters from old army buddies and stray Christmas cards to more than twenty years' worth of Theater at Monmouth programs. The memory of how much Gramps had enjoyed his regular doses of Shakespeare every summer brought a fleeting smile to Ariadne's face.

As she sat, legs curled under her, on the floor in front of the desk, Ariadne felt very close to her grandfather. It seemed to her that he was there with her, guiding her hand as she sifted through the contents of his desk. She was about to start returning items to the bottom

drawer when she realized that it wasn't empty after all.
An envelope, smudged and yellowed with age, lay
squarely in the center, almost as if it had been placed
there after she'd removed everything else.

Don't be foolish, she chided herself, but when she
caught sight of the return address she shivered. There
was something eerie about finding a letter from her
father just now.

She did not remember him and couldn't recall ever
having seen his handwriting before, but it was his name
in the upper left-hand corner. Mark Palmer. And the
address beneath was a post office box…in Florida.

Once she had the envelope in her hands, Ariadne
hesitated, suddenly not at all certain that she wanted to
know what was inside. Gramps had always led her to
believe that her parents were Maine natives who'd
never ventured out of state but once. That had been to
take a fateful automobile trip to Boston, one which had
ended in a fiery crash and killed them both.

He'd lied, at least about part of the story. The date
on the postmark was clear even all these years later.
This letter had been mailed to Gramps from Tarpon
Springs, Florida…just one week after Ariadne's birth.

She felt a tingle of trepidation as she turned the envelope over and lifted the flap. She tried to convince
herself that she'd just misunderstood Gramps, who had
always been reluctant to speak of his son. The pained
look that appeared on his face every time Mark's name
was mentioned had been enough to discourage the
young Ariadne from asking too many questions.

So, Mark Palmer might have made trips out of state
all the time, and he might have had any number of
reasons to visit Florida. And he'd probably left his wife
and new baby behind.

Expecting a letter, Ariadne was startled to discover that the envelope contained only a snapshot. It slid out into her hand facedown, so that she read the inscription on the back before she saw the corresponding image on the front.

"Pop," her father had written in the same messy scrawl that he'd used to address the envelope. "First shot of your twin granddaughters."

Her hands suddenly as unsteady as her breathing, Ariadne carefully turned the photograph over. It *was* her father. She'd seen pictures of him even if there hadn't been any of her mother. There was no mistaking, either, the fact that he was holding two identical bundles in his arms. Ariadne began to tremble, shaking so hard that she dropped the photograph.

"No," she whispered.

She was an only child. Gramps had always said so. Both fists clenched convulsively as tears began to flow down her pale cheeks.

Gramps had lied.

And Clay Franklin had been telling the truth.

Clay was about to knock at Ariadne's door when he heard the muffled sound of a woman weeping.

"Ariadne?" He didn't wait for an invitation to enter her apartment. The door was unlocked and opened directly into the living room.

Arms wrapped around herself, she was kneeling on the floor, head bent. She looked up when he repeated her name, but instead of being frightened, or even angry that he'd barged in, she just stared at him. Against the darkness of her hair and eyes her pale face was doubly alarming. Although Clay had no idea what had brought it on, his first thought was that she was in shock.

Kicking the door closed behind him, discarding his gloves and jacket as he went, he crossed the short distance between them, hauled her to her feet and gathered her into his arms.

"It's okay, honey," he murmured, stroking her back and gently maneuvering her toward a nearby sofa. By the time they reached it, she was clinging to him and crying uncontrollably. He marveled at how soft she was, at how right it felt to hold her cradled against his chest.

He'd been on his way back to the bed and breakfast after dinner out when he'd impulsively decided to have one more try at convincing Ariadne that he was telling the truth. He hadn't counted on finding her in distress, nor had he anticipated how he would feel toward her once he held her nestled close in his embrace. It was an odd combination, both protective and predatory.

"I'll take care of you," Clay heard himself promise. "I'll take care of everything."

Pretend she's Fay, he warned himself. But Ariadne's body was pressed intimately against his own. Holding Fay close while she cried over some teenaged trauma had not prepared him for this.

Get a grip, he warned himself. He might want Ariadne, but that didn't mean he had to do anything about his desire. Tempting as it was to contemplate soothing her distress by making love to her, that was not an option.

Not even if she did make his blood sing and his heart soar.

Chapter Three

Eventually, Ariadne's crying shuddered to a halt. With a gulp and a final sob she lifted her head. Her eyes widened as she recognized him. "You."

"Me," he agreed. Had she been expecting someone else? Was that why the door had been left unlocked?

Momentarily annoyed at the idea that she might have another man in her life, even though Duncan had found no evidence of a lover, Clay tightened his grip on her shoulders.

Her expression reflected first confusion and then embarrassment. When Ariadne began to squirm, Clay reluctantly released her. She scooted away from him, all the way to the far end of the sofa, where she fumbled for the box of tissues on the end table. With a noisy trumpeting, she blew her nose, which was already shiny and red from all the weeping.

Clay couldn't contain a small smile. Unlike Fay, Ariadne let her passions have full rein. Her hair, which had come loose from its severe style, now fell in untidy clumps around her tearstained face. The effect should have been unappealing, but somehow, on Ariadne, dishevelment made her seem more desirable. Clay's fantasy, the one about seeing those long ebony strands completely free of confinement, expanded to picture her hair spread out on a silk pillowcase.

Either she sensed his reaction and took offense or she truly didn't care how she looked. As soon as she rallied she challenged him. "What are you doing here?" she demanded. "The bookstore closed hours ago."

"I came to talk to you," Clay said patiently. "You know very well that the bookstore has nothing to do with what's between us."

"I'm not interested in talking."

It was on the tip of his tongue to ask what else she might be interested in doing, but he caught himself in time. He might not have met Shanna yet, but he knew the child must be asleep in the next room.

"Now seems as good a time as any," he said mildly.

"Now is a terrible time. Any time would be a terrible time. I don't want to hear anything you have to say, anyway, so you might as well just leave."

Once again she pawed at the tissue box, but this time she came up empty. Her lower lip trembled, as if this small setback might just be the final straw.

Clay offered her his handkerchief. She snatched it and wiped her eyes. Then she caught sight of his shoulder and gasped. "I've ruined your shirt."

"The shirt isn't important." It had a large damp spot. That was all. Clay frowned as he studied her stricken expression. She still looked dazed, and her face was too pale, which made her seem fragile and in need of care. "Do you have any liquor in the place? Brandy?"

"You want a drink?"

At her genuine puzzlement, he shot an exasperated look in her direction, then got up to see for himself. "I don't need a drink. You do."

"I don't drink."

In her minuscule kitchen he began to rummage through the cabinets. When they yielded nothing of any use, he checked the contents of the refrigerator. A few minutes later he returned to the living room carrying a brimming, clinking glass, an offering she eyed with suspicion.

"What's that?"

"The best I could do. Bottled water. On ice." He pressed the cold drink into her hand, his fingers closing around hers to force them into a proper grip. "It will be easier on you to take a few swallows voluntarily than to argue with me."

Glaring at him over the rim of the glass, she complied with his wishes.

"Good girl. Now, why don't you tell me what this is all about?"

Ariadne sighed. She didn't look happy about having him there, but she'd obviously realized that he wasn't going to leave until he'd gotten some answers. "I suppose you could say I just got a message from beyond the grave."

"A psychic experience of some sort?" Making no effort to hide his skepticism, he sat down next to her again.

"Not exactly." Her glass hit the coffee table with a thump that sent water sloshing every which way. "This is crazy," she muttered, annoyed at her own lack of control. Her hands were still shaking badly. "I never go to pieces like this. I'm sorry about your shirt."

"Will you forget the damn shirt? Talk to me, Ariadne. Maybe I can help."

She closed her eyes for a few seconds, then opened them to give him a long, surprisingly steady look. "Maybe not. Maybe you're the last person I should talk to right now."

"Give me a break, honey. I'm worried about you. When I first came in here you looked like you were about to pass out."

"I'd have been fine. You just caught me at a bad moment."

"Uh-huh. That's why you came into my arms like a long-lost lover and opened the floodgates."

When a violent red blush flowed up her neck and into her face, he felt a surge of pleasure. "Much better. Dead white is not your color."

"I just...overreacted."

"To what?"

Ariadne took a deep, steadying breath. "I suppose you might as well know." She gestured toward the clutter that surrounded the desk. "I found an old envelope in my grandfather's things, an envelope with a photograph inside. I'm willing to swear I never saw that envelope before. I know I never saw the picture. And yet I used to play with everything in that desk. Everything else was familiar to me. So, for a moment it seemed to me that the thing had just materialized out of thin air." She gave a nervous laugh. "Or that it was...sent."

Resting one hand on her forearm, hoping she'd take comfort from the small gesture, Clay watched her gather her thoughts. He was beginning to have an inkling of what this was all about, and to understand why she'd said that he was the last one she wanted to talk to right now.

Too bad. He was here, and he was already involved. He gave her a few more moments to collect herself, then squeezed gently and used his grip to pull her to her feet alongside him.

"Show me the picture, Ariadne."

"It was right there." She indicated the patch of bare carpet in front of the desk where she'd been kneeling when he arrived. An edge of panic laced her voice. "I don't see it anywhere now. Do you think I could have imagined it?" This last sounded hopeful.

"I think you dropped it. Come on. Let's look for it." He kept his hand lightly touching the small of her back to steady her as she reluctantly retraced her path across the room. There was no immediate sign of either photograph or envelope.

Blinking hard, as if she was determined not to cry again, Ariadne clutched the top of the desk for support. "Oh, Lord! Maybe I did hallucinate the whole thing! The possibility of some sort of psychic experience was bad enough, but if I've started seeing things..."

"Take it easy, Ariadne." His gaze swept over the piles she'd been making of papers and memorabilia and then over the open drawer. He discounted her psychic theory easily enough. The envelope she'd found had probably just been stuck to something else, keeping her from noticing it earlier.

Clay's visual survey of the area around them turned up only one photograph. Hanging on the wall next to the desk in a silver frame was an eight-by-ten of a small child held in the arms of a rail-thin, gray-haired man with a deeply lined face and gnarled fingers. Obviously Shanna and, he presumed, Edward Palmer.

The dark blue carpet softened her landing as Ariadne sank to her hands and knees and began to search under the furniture for the missing items. Her muffled cry of triumph drew Clay's attention back to her just in time to catch a glimpse of a shapely derriere wiggling backward toward him.

Desire's sharp talons gripped him in the moment before she came up to her knees and swiveled to face him, the missing snapshot and envelope clutched tightly in one slightly grubby fist. With her free hand she shoved several tangled strands of hair out of her face.

"Thank goodness. I'm not crazy." And then the flush of success faded as she remembered all that finding this particular photo meant. "I'm not crazy," she said again, bitterly. "I've just lived a lie for my entire life."

Unable to deny it, even if he'd wanted to, Clay reached for the faded snapshot. He read the inscription, then turned it over to look at infants he recognized instantly. He'd seen a picture very similar to this particular photo, only in his it had been the twins' mother holding them. The reminder helped him get his raging hormones back under control.

"You and Fay. You were just a few days old when this was taken."

The starch seemed to go out of Ariadne's knees. She sank back against the side of the desk. Her small victory in locating the photograph had paled beside the enormity of all its existence meant. Crumpling the envelope in her hand with sudden savagery, she would have flung it away if Clay hadn't caught her wrist. He removed the damning evidence, then settled himself beside her on the soft, deep pile carpet and slipped one arm around her shoulders.

"Cry if you want to."

"No. I'm past that."

He smoothed the envelope out and noted the Florida postmark. "If you'd like to talk, I'm a good listener."

"I just can't understand it." There was a catch in her voice, but she did manage to head off new tears. "Why, Clay? Why did Gramps lie to me? Why tell me I was born here in Augusta, the only child of parents who died in a car crash on the one occasion in their whole lives when they decided to take an out-of-state vacation?"

"We may never know," Clay told her, though he still subscribed to the theory that Edward Palmer had been afraid of losing custody of his granddaughter.

"There's no question now," Ariadne admitted with a deep sigh. "That man in the photograph is my father. I've never seen a picture of my mother but there were other pictures of him. But I don't...I just can't..."

Silence stretched between them, lengthening until Clay couldn't tolerate it any longer. He stood slowly and once again pulled her to her feet beside him. Without quite knowing how it happened, his arms were wrapped around her.

Desire coursed through him in a wave thick and hot as a lava flow. He recognized an answering heat in Ariadne's eyes before they drifted slowly closed. She swayed toward him.

Clay caught himself a millisecond before he gave in to the urge to find out if her lips were as soft as they looked. He came very close to forgetting all about conflict of interest, honor, common sense. It would have been so easy to take advantage of Ariadne in her present confused state, to yield to the urging of his painfully aroused body, to give her as much pleasure as having her would give him.

It would also be unforgivable. *She has a child,* he thought a little desperately, adding one more reason to an already-lengthy list.

Getting involved with a woman with a child was never a good idea. He'd seen too many innocents hurt by a parent's incessant search for the right mate. An affair could be just as traumatic for the child as a short, failed marriage. Clay had no intention of indulging in either. He'd almost managed to force himself to release Ariadne when a small voice called out to her from the other room.

"Mommy," Shanna asked, "is that Bumpa?"

Ariadne's eyes flew open, wide with shock.

Clay had already let her go. "Bumpa?"

"Her great-grandfather. She must have thought... She heard a male voice. I—" Ariadne abruptly gave up any effort to explain and left Clay in order to go to her daughter.

He stared after her, beset by the uneasy suspicion that he was in young Shanna's debt. He wanted to believe he'd have acted honorably on his own, but he wasn't convinced of it. Ariadne Palmer had a powerful effect on him. He was going to have to be very careful around her from now on.

"I'm sorry about this, Laurie," Ariadne said as she and Shanna entered the bookstore the next morning. Not only was she late getting to work, but she had a sobbing child in tow.

"What's the matter?"

"Your guess is as good as mine."

Laurie lifted a brow. Ariadne shrugged. Shanna had refused to go to day care and Ariadne hadn't had the heart to insist. Her daughter's tantrums were rare, but they were real doozies when they did occur. Although she knew she shouldn't give in to what amounted to emotional blackmail, Ariadne just wasn't up to a fight with Shanna. Not after all that had happened last night.

Tears still streamed down the little girl's face. Ariadne had to fight a temptation to tell her to dry up, that she'd won. No one had ever claimed that motherhood was easy. But before she could decide what approach to take with Shanna, the door chimes sounded to herald Clay Franklin's arrival.

Ariadne had been dreading seeing him again. She was embarrassed that she'd allowed herself to cry in his arms. Now he was going to see Shanna in a similar state, which for some inexplicable reason bothered her even more.

"I've brought you a present," he said to Ariadne. He didn't seem to notice that Shanna had ducked behind Ariadne's skirts as soon as he came in and was now peering cautiously up at him from her hiding place.

"I don't want anything from you," she told him.

"Not even a photograph of Phyllis Allandale?" He held out a plain manila envelope.

Shanna emerged from cover, her tears miraculously gone. "What did you bring me?" she asked Clay.

"Shanna!"

But Clay chuckled and knelt down beside Ariadne's daughter. "Hello, Shanna. My name is Clay. I didn't bring you anything because I didn't know you'd be here."

One huge leftover tear rolled down her cheek. "I'm supposed to be in school."

"Hey, don't turn on the waterworks!" He lifted Shanna up onto the counter, which kept her at eye level with him. "The way you're carrying on, you'll have me thinking that nobody loves you."

Shanna considered this a moment, then sniffed loudly. "No. Everybody loves me."

"Four-year-olds have no modesty," Ariadne told him.

Clay was good with kids. She hadn't expected him to be. She wasn't sure what to make of the discovery, either, and when an obvious explanation occurred to her, she blurted out a question before she could stop herself. "Do you have children of your own?"

His answer was delivered in a light, bantering tone, but Ariadne heard the conviction behind it. "No kids. No wife. Never have had. Never will."

"I'm staying here today," Shanna announced, tugging at Clay's sleeve to regain his attention.

"I can see that," he said. "Are you going to help your mother mind the store?"

Shanna nodded so vigorously that her curls danced.

"How about you help me for a little while first," Laurie suggested. "I have a great big pile of books in the other room that need to be put on the shelves."

"Okay, Aunt Laurie." Shanna reached out to Clay to be lifted down. As soon as he obliged, she was off and running, her earlier agitation completely forgotten.

Clay waited until both Shanna and Laurie were out of earshot before he turned to Ariadne. "If it was my being in your apartment last night that upset her, I'm sorry."

His visit had upset someone in that apartment, Ariadne thought, but it hadn't been Shanna. "It wasn't just you. She'd had a bad dream. My grandfather was very good with her when that happened. We spent a lot of weekends with him."

Was she making any sense? Ariadne wondered. And she also wondered why it should matter so much to her that Clay understand. "Shanna has a hard time dealing with his death. Sometimes she convinces herself that Bumpa just went away for a while."

The lack of expression on Clay's face confused her. He seemed to be trying to distance himself from her, an effort she supposed she ought to approve of. Instead, his aloof behavior just made her remember, with lingering regret, how good it had felt to be held tight in his arms.

"Aren't you going to take a look at the photographs?" Clay indicated the envelope she still held.

"Yes. Of course."

Fumbling a little, she ripped it open. There were several pictures inside, but the one on top caught and held her attention. This was the first time she'd seen a likeness of her mother, but the face in front of her was very familiar. Phyllis Allandale's daughters might not resemble her...but her granddaughter did.

"I always thought Shanna must take after her father's family," Ariadne murmured.

"Apparently not." Clay took the envelope and the remaining photographs from her nerveless fingers and extracted one, placing it on the counter. "You and Fay resemble Phyllis's mother, Lila."

A slender, dark-haired woman stared back at Ariadne. Next to her was a nattily dressed, distinguished-looking man with a decidedly forbidding expression on his square-jawed face. He was older than his wife, but hardly the doddering senior citizen she'd been expecting to see. Ariadne told herself that this must not be a very recent photograph.

There were three other photos. The first was similar to the one she'd found the night before. The other two showed Fay at Shanna's age, alone in one shot and with Phyllis in the other.

I could have been in that picture, Ariadne thought as she added the latter to the family album now spread out on the countertop. *If Gramps had contacted the Allandales when my father died, I'd have gotten to know my mother.*

But would Gramps himself still have been in her life if he had? That question had haunted Ariadne during the darkest hours of the night. If Clay's theory was correct, then it didn't say anything good about these newly discovered relatives. Gramps had feared they'd take her away from him. After seeing George Allandale's hard features, she suspected Gramps might have been right.

Ariadne didn't want to pursue that line of thought. She didn't want to think about the Allandales at all. She wanted to go back to the way things had been before Clay Franklin walked into her life. Another small sigh escaped her. What she wanted no longer mattered.

"When are you going to tell Shanna?" Clay asked.

"Tell her what?"

"That she still has one great-grandfather left. That she has an aunt and a great-grandmother. That you're going to Florida to meet them."

"It's too soon to tell her anything. I haven't even decided if *I* want to meet them yet."

"They're her family. Your family."

"They're strangers. Why should I trust them around my daughter just because they're related to us by blood? If what you've told me is true, these grandparents in Florida have known all along that I existed somewhere. They never tried to find me. And my own mother gave me away, promised never to see me again. What kind of person could do that?"

"Your father agreed to the same conditions."

"He died when I was three. Perhaps, if he'd lived—"

"But he didn't. And your grandfather never tried to reunite you with the rest of your family, either."

"Maybe he didn't know where to find them." She clung to that thought, still reluctant to accept that the man who'd raised her had deliberately lied.

"There's not much point in rehashing the past," Clay said after a moment. "It's the future you need to be concerned about now. Shanna's future."

He'd put some distance between them with his stiff, formal bearing, and Ariadne was glad of it. But everything was still happening too fast. She couldn't cope with any more right now.

"Don't push me, Clay," she warned.

Accurately assessing her mood, he changed tactics. "Would it help to ask me questions about your family? I'll tell you all I can."

He wasn't going to go away. And there seemed little point in delaying the inevitable, beyond having a chance to collect her wits. She wasn't going to go to Florida or anywhere else with him unless she was sure it was the best thing to do, but how could she decide that if she didn't have more answers?

"It might," she told Clay. She was about to ask him to tell her more about her twin when footsteps at a run warned her Shanna was on her way back. "I don't want Shanna to know anything about this yet. We can talk while she takes her nap."

"All right," he agreed.

The child was already there, tugging at her mother's skirt to drag her over to a small grouping of Queen Anne chairs. "Tell me a mommy story, Mommy."

"A mommy story?" His interest caught, Clay leaned back against the counter, prepared to listen, too.

"The one about the piano," Shanna said.

A small, self-conscious smile on her face because Clay was there, Ariadne shrugged, transferred her attention to her daughter, and launched into what was clearly an oft-told tale. It began "Once upon a time" but she was recounting something that had happened to her as a child. She and two friends, Lynn and Yvonne, were trying to think of ways to get Ariadne out of performing in a piano recital. Clay had no trouble identifying. He'd hated those things himself.

"And Lynn said..." Ariadne paused and let her daughter finish the sentence.

"You could break a finger!" Childish giggles accompanied the outrageous suggestion.

Ariadne cast another sheepish glance in Clay's direction. "I was terrified about playing in front of an audience," she explained, a trace of defensiveness in her voice. "I had good reason to be, too. The recital piece my piano teacher picked out for me was a beast. Loaded with sixteenth notes. I was sure I was going to butcher the song in front of Gramps and all our friends."

"I assume you didn't really break a finger."

"No. I was too chicken to do that. Luckily, I was able to come up with a better solution. I walked out onto that stage and instead of sitting down at the piano I turned to the crowd and announced that I wasn't going to play my recital piece. I was going to play my favorite song from the first-year piano book instead, because I liked it better, and because I could play it better, too.''

"Good for you," Clay said. He wished he'd thought of doing that in a similar situation.

"I almost lost my nerve," Ariadne admitted. "I can still remember how quickly I sat down on that piano bench, before I could change my mind. But then, it was the oddest thing. Once I started to play, I wasn't nervous anymore. I stopped worrying about whether I hit the right keys or not and, when I got to the end of the song, I realized it was over much too soon. Instead of stopping, I went right into the recital piece, sixteenth notes and all, and played it through without a hitch.''

"Mommy did good," Shanna said. "She was a brave little girl."

Grinning, Clay agreed, but his smile faded fast when he realized he'd lost his objectivity again. Last night, it had felt entirely too right to comfort Ariadne. Now he'd gone and fallen under her daughter's elfin spell. Together, they were a dangerous combination.

Keep a safe emotional distance, he warned himself. *Concentrate on business.* The sooner he convinced Ariadne to meet with the Allandales, the sooner his own life could return to normal.

He stuck to that resolve for all of four hours, until he let himself in through the front door of Laurie's house, where Ariadne had asked him to meet her "on neutral ground." The unmistakable sounds of an argument in progress drew him along the hallway. Raised voices, one male and one female, were coming from the old-fashioned parlor.

"You're taking child support from me," the man accused. "All I want is a look at her to see what I'm paying for."

"You didn't want anything to do with your daughter when she was born," Ariadne answered. "You have no rights where she's concerned. None at all."

Brad Comfort, Clay deduced as he paused in the opening between the pocket doors. He disliked the man on sight.

Laurie shushed the two of them. "If you don't pipe down, you're going to wake Shanna. She's upstairs taking a nap."

"She's here?" Comfort started for the staircase only to find Clay blocking his way. They were close to the same height and Brad Comfort was in good physical shape, but Clay refused to budge.

"Not a good idea to try to see Shanna without her mother's permission," he warned. "And it's Laurie's house."

"Who the hell are you?"

"Clay is a friend," Laurie said quickly. Ariadne seemed at a loss for words. "And he's right, Brad. You may be my cousin, but you can't just go barging around in my house as if you owned it."

"Perhaps you'd like to tell us all why you're suddenly so interested in the girl?" An instinct born of too many divorce and custody cases provoked Clay's gravest suspicions about Brad Comfort. There had been several judgments just lately awarding a working mother's child to a father whose second wife stayed home full-time. He didn't borrow trouble by mentioning that worst-case scenario to Ariadne, but he decided it wouldn't hurt to have Duncan ask a few more questions about Brad Comfort.

"I don't give a damn about the kid." Comfort's nasty tone of voice added fuel to Clay's dislike. "It's my wife who's curious." With that troubling declaration, he slammed out of the house.

"This is all your fault." Ariadne turned on Clay, glaring.

"Mine? Why?"

"If it hadn't been for your private investigator's snooping, Brad's brand-new bride would never even have known Shanna existed."

Guilty as charged, Clay couldn't think of a single thing to say in his own defense.

As soon as she saw Shanna off to day care on Friday morning, Ariadne stuck her head into the bookstore to let Laurie know she was leaving.

"What do I tell Clay when he comes in?" Laurie asked.

"That I'm not here."

Clay Franklin's persistence was exasperating, the more so since she genuinely enjoyed some aspects of having him around. Enjoyed them too much, perhaps.

They'd both pulled back after their emotional encounter in her apartment. Neither wanted the barriers to come down that far again. And she'd been furious with him that afternoon in Laurie's parlor. And yet there was something about him that appealed to her, something that made her think about him more than she wanted to, especially late at night.

Yesterday he'd spent almost the entire day with her while she worked, answering at least a few of her questions about Fay and the Allandales. He'd evaded others, saying she'd see for herself when she met them.

They'd talked about other things, too, and discovered that they both liked cheerful old movie musicals, especially those made from Broadway plays. So did Fay, apparently. Fay, however, did not care for taking long walks in the autumn, to look at the foliage, and Clay and Ariadne did.

Would she still have any contact with Clay Franklin come fall? Ariadne couldn't begin to guess.

"Tell him I had to get away from his constant lobbying to get me to agree to go to Florida," she said aloud. The accusation wasn't entirely unfounded.

"There's an easier way to get him to stop. Give in."

"It's not that simple."

"He's not married."

"You heard him the other day—'No kids. No wife. Never have had. Never will.' The man's not interested in marriage. Neither am I," she added quickly.

"There are other possibilities."

"Forget it, Laurie. Yes, I'm attracted to him, but he's all wrong for me." She tried for a lighter note. "Aside from everything else, he lives in Connecticut."

"Connecticut. Florida. Who cares? Leave Maine for a change. Take a little vacation time and broaden your horizons."

"I'm not about to go away and leave you shorthanded," Ariadne said firmly.

"You're taking today off," Laurie pointed out.

"That's different. It's just one day. Not even the whole day, either." But the reminder that she had to be somewhere in an hour gave Ariadne the excuse she needed to escape an increasingly uncomfortable conversation. "The car must be warmed up by now. Got to go."

"Say hi to Miss Emily for me," Laurie called as Ariadne opened the door and let in a blast of arctic air.

Head down, both to watch her footing and to keep her face from freezing, Ariadne had almost reached her eight-year-old, four-wheel-drive station wagon before she realized it was occupied. The cold snap that had necessitated warming up the engine had also given Clay Franklin time to install himself in the vehicle. Already buckled up, he gave her a lopsided grin.

"What do you think you're doing?" she demanded as she slid in on the driver's side and hurriedly closed the door behind her. The interior was blessedly warm. Maybe too warm, she decided as she swiveled around to face her uninvited passenger.

"This looked like it might be a good place to talk to you without interruptions from customers. How about I ride along with you to wherever you're going?"

"You don't give me much choice," she grumbled. It would take a forklift to evict him. "Anyone ever tell you that you're awfully high-handed?"

"Yes. Your sister."

She turned away, closing her eyes for a moment. There was no way today was going to be easy, but Clay's presence wouldn't affect the outcome one way or the other. She knew from experience that he could be downright comforting in a crisis, though she didn't think it wise to dwell on that notion just now.

"Ground rules," she said, sending a sharp, narrow-eyed look in his direction. No way would she spend the next hour listening to him plead his case. "We don't discuss family until after...until later."

"That sounds a bit ominous."

"Do you agree?"

"You don't give me much choice," he said, throwing her own words back at her. "You're the one in the driver's seat."

It seemed likely to Ariadne that what she discovered during the next few hours would determine whether or not she ever agreed to meet her sister and the older Allandales. Given that, she supposed she might as well take Clay along.

At least this way she wouldn't have to waste time afterward in explaining her decision. She and Clay would learn the truth at the same time.

She felt oddly comforted by the fact that they'd be together when she found out the real reason Gramps had told her all those family lies.

Chapter Four

They left the city and headed west into the mountains. After Clay polished off the steaming cup of coffee and two doughnuts they'd stopped for at a drive-through doughnut shop on the way out of Augusta, he simply relaxed and enjoyed the view. It was a perfect day for a drive in the country—clear and cold. Snow lent brilliance to the landscape, but was thankfully absent from the road.

"So," he said as he tucked his napkin into the empty cup and deposited it in her trash bag. "Where are we going?"

"To a *Boston Post* cane ceremony."

She didn't need to elaborate. As a native New Englander, Clay knew what she was talking about. The passing of the *Boston Post* cane was a tradition that was alive and well in many communities, even though the old *Boston Post* newspaper had gone out of business decades ago. The original canes had been distributed to hundreds of New England towns, given to each one's oldest living citizen with the stipulation that it be transmitted, upon death, to the next oldest person in that town.

"Who's the honoree?" he asked.

"It's being presented to Miss Emily Vaughan," Ariadne told him. A fond smile played around her mouth and she relaxed a bit. "Miss Emily is an old family friend. She's also the one responsible for getting me interested in book collecting. When I turned twelve, she brought me a huge box full of books. There were twenty-five volumes inside, the entire Beverly Gray series."

"Beverly Gray?"

"Think Nancy Drew, only earlier. Miss Emily collected all the girls' books of the thirties and forties and the Beverly Grays were her favorites."

"She must have thought a lot of you, then, to give them to you."

Clay watched her, fascinated, as she began to reminisce. This was really the first time she'd opened up and let herself talk to him about her past. They'd both been careful not to get too personal since that night in her apartment.

He'd also avoided saying much about the Allandales, in part because he was reluctant to take the chance of revealing their true financial status. Ariadne had been equally wary of discussing her late grandfather.

For all that, they'd found plenty to talk about, and he'd continued to enjoy her company entirely too much. He even liked her daughter, who was bright and talkative and a natural flirt.

"In the series," Ariadne said, "Beverly and her

friend Lenora work for a newspaper and solve mysteries in their spare time.''

"Did you identify with Beverly?"

"Nope. Lenora. She had a job as a news photographer and for a long while I thought photography would be an ideal career for me. Turned out I wasn't all that good at it, but I did work my way through college as a stringer for a local paper. I'd get called out in the middle of the night to take pictures of traffic accidents. After four years of that, I'd had enough. Now I just take pictures for fun.''

She was full of surprises, Clay thought. The fact that Ariadne had worked her way through college shed further doubt on the story Duncan had gotten from Brad Comfort and his mother. The more Clay got to know Ariadne for himself, the more he began to doubt that material wealth mattered much to her. Laurie had let it slip that every penny of Shanna's child support went into a savings account in the little girl's name.

Clay wished he'd never made that promise to George. He didn't like the fact that he was trying to convince Ariadne to visit Florida under false pretenses. The sooner she agreed to go, though, the sooner his deception would be over. "You know, Ariadne," he began in a carefully casual voice, "it only seems fair, since I'm going on this little trip with you, that you reconsider taking one with me. There are flights leaving Portland every day. There's even one that goes direct to Tampa.''

Her hands tightened on the wheel, but she kept her tone light. "You agreed not to nag me if I let you come along," she reminded him.

A few moments later, she signaled a right turn and

drove along a tree-lined street toward the center of a very small town. "Welcome to Geneva."

Clay glanced at the name painted above the door of the tiny post office they were passing, lifting an eyebrow at her pronunciation. "Jen-uh-ver?" he echoed. It was spelled Geneva, as in Switzerland. "Why the accent on the first syllable?"

"You're in Maine. We put the accent on the first syllable in Madrid, too."

"And the 'r' sound at the end of Geneva? Where did that come from?"

Straight-faced, she quipped, "I expect it's one of the *r*'s that got dropped from Bah Hahbah."

He was still shaking his head over her exaggerated accent when she parked in front of a three-story brick house and got out of the station wagon. Pausing only long enough to extract a 35mm camera from the back seat, she led the way inside.

At least two dozen people were gathered in the nursing home's old-fashioned parlor. Since the ceremony was just starting, Ariadne didn't have an opportunity to introduce Clay to Miss Emily but he had no difficulty picking her out in the crowd. Miss Emily Vaughan was a tiny lady, all pink and white, from her neatly permed snowy hair and rosy cheeks to a chiffon dress that struck Clay as being more suitable for a 1957 prom queen than for the elderly woman enthroned on a straight-backed chair. She even had a corsage of pink and white carnations.

Clearing his throat, a rotund, nervous-looking man in a three-piece suit began to speak in portentous tones. "In ninety-seven years, Amelia Vaughan—"

"Emily," someone whispered loudly.

"In ninety-seven years, Emily Vaughan, you have

seen many changes. You are a valuable resource for our community and an historian of tremendous caliber. It is my honor and privilege as town manager to present you with this cane honoring Geneva's oldest citizen.''

On the second try, he managed to pronounce Geneva like a native. Muffled sniggers accompanied the scattered applause. Miss Emily simply curled her gnarled fingers possessively around the shaft of the ebony cane and tilted it so that light coming in through the windows glinted off the elaborately decorated gold head, momentarily blinding the officious town manager.

Ariadne stepped forward, her camera raised. "Say cheese," she ordered.

A young man who wore a badge identifying him as a reporter for the local paper took several pictures, too. As soon as they were done, the town manager's phony political smile vanished. "Why wasn't there a video crew here from Channel 6 News?" he demanded. "They showed up the last time."

"The last recipient was 104," Miss Emily said bluntly. She gave him a smile as phony as his own. "I'm sure you'll have a very nice picture in the *Weekly Register*." She waited until he'd made a hasty exit to add, not quite under her breath, "Pompous skunk-hunter!"

Puzzled, Clay looked to Ariadne for a translation.

"Out-of-stater," she whispered as she left his side to give Miss Emily an affectionate hug.

"Who's he?" The old woman's birdlike gaze fixed on Clay.

Ariadne introduced him, then added, "He's a friend. Be nice to him."

Clay bent forward to shake a surprisingly strong

hand. Lilac-scented cologne drifted his way. "I am delighted to meet you, Miss Emily."

"You're not from around here, are you, dear?"

"No, ma'am. I'm sorry to say I'm not a native Mainer."

"As long as you're sorry about it, you'll do."

"Miss Emily," Ariadne said cautiously, "is not a relative, but she was my father's godmother. She and my grandmother Palmer were very good friends."

The old woman smoothed one hand over the knob on her *Boston Post* cane. "I was her Sunday school teacher first, then her friend, when the difference in our ages no longer made so much difference. I was close friends with Edward Palmer, too." She chuckled. "I used to tell him that if I'd been twenty years younger I'd have married him myself. He always thought I was joking."

"May I tell you a story, Miss Emily?" Clay asked. He'd been right to suspect Ariadne of harboring ulterior motives, but in this case they'd turned out to be good ones.

The elderly woman's eyes glittered, convincing him that underneath that tight perm there was still a first-rate brain. With a few choice words, she cleared everyone else out of the parlor.

"Start at the beginning," she ordered as soon as Clay and Ariadne were seated on the sofa across from her. It sagged a bit, throwing them together. They both pretended to ignore the pressure of hip and thigh even when Miss Emily gave them a knowing look.

Ten minutes later, Clay had summarized most of what he'd told Ariadne, and she'd produced the photograph she'd found in her grandfather's things for Miss Emily's inspection. A deep sadness came into those sharp old eyes as she studied the snapshot. Her arthritic hands trembled as she handed it back.

"He hoped you'd never have to know any of this," she told Ariadne. "He tried very hard to forget what really happened. I suspect that after a while he even managed to convince himself that what he'd told you was the truth." Miss Emily went on to confirm that Mark Palmer had gone to college in Florida. "He dropped out after he married. Upset Edward doing that, but not as much as the divorce did."

Clay started to comment, then thought better of it.

"Why didn't Gramps try to find my mother after my father died?" Ariadne asked.

"He didn't think much of her or her folk. After all, she agreed to that divorce, too. What kind of mother gives up a child? Not that he wasn't glad Mark got you, mind."

Tears shimmered in Ariadne's eyes. "Why did he have to lie to me?"

Her broken whisper touched Clay's heart. Helplessly he looked to Miss Emily for guidance. After one sharp glance, she ignored him, concentrating on Ariadne.

"He loved you, girl. Never forget that. Anything he did was because he wanted what was best for you."

"So he decided to deceive me?"

"He didn't want to risk losing you."

"He *lied* to me."

Miss Emily's whole body seemed to slump. Clay was afraid she might topple right out of her chair, but she righted herself, glared at him and then addressed Ariadne. "This is too much for an old woman. I'm plumb tired out. Be a good girl, Ariadne, and help me up to my room. I think I'd best lie down for a spell."

"But Clay—"

"Clay can wait for you in the car," he offered, and earned a beaming smile of approval from Miss Emily.

"What was that all about?" Ariadne demanded a few minutes later. Miss Emily's exhaustion had vanished the moment Clay had left the parlor.

"No reason to let that flatlander in on everything." She closed the door behind them and continued at a painful snail's pace toward the far side of her small bedroom.

"I wanted Clay to hear what you had to say."

"Not enough, apparently, to tell him I'd already heard some of the story from you when we spoke on the telephone last night."

Caught out, Ariadne fidgeted like a naughty child. She had asked Miss Emily, when the older woman called to remind her about the *Boston Post* cane ceremony, if she knew anything about the Allandales. Miss Emily had asked a few questions of her own, then refused to give Ariadne any answers until they could speak in person.

"You said you had something to show me," Ariadne reminded her. "And you promised to answer all my questions."

"So I do and so I will, but there's no need for an outsider to hear more." She'd made her way to an old-fashioned chiffonier and opened one of the drawers. Now she turned, two envelopes in her hand. "Edward left two letters in my keeping. One for you and one for Phaedra."

Ariadne abruptly sat down on the edge of the bed. "Just one surprise after another," she muttered as her vision blurred. She was really getting tired of this tendency to tear up at the slightest provocation, too. "Why didn't you give them to me before this?"

"You didn't know you had a sister. Why open up a can of worms?" Miss Emily placed the two business-size envelopes next to Ariadne on the handmade quilt.

Ariadne had to clear her throat before she could get any words out. She picked up the letter her grandfather had left for her and turned it over and over in her hands, but she didn't open it. She wasn't sure she wanted to. She wasn't sure of anything anymore.

"I'm having a lot of trouble with this, Miss Emily. What if Clay had never come looking for me? I'd *never* have known the truth."

"What-ifs are a waste of time. Seems to me you ought to be delighted to find out you're not a poor little orphan girl anymore."

"Would Gramps have been happy if I'd found out while he was still living?"

"He'd have been happy if Mark had finished college and found a nice Maine girl to marry, but that's neither here nor there. Are you going to read that or not? I never thought you were a coward, Ariadne." She held out a letter opener that had a mother-of-pearl handle.

Reluctantly, Ariadne slit the envelope, unfolded the letter her grandfather had left for her and began to read. She couldn't take everything in at once, but one line stood out. "I had a good reason for keeping things from you," he'd written. "If you decide you must try to make contact with your mother, be careful."

Ariadne was a long time settling Miss Emily, but Clay had expected her to be. He wasn't surprised, either, by her subdued demeanor when she finally returned to the station wagon. "Do you want me to drive back?"

Nodding, she lapsed into a contemplative silence as soon as the car pulled away from the curb.

"It's no good brooding about what Miss Emily told you," Clay remarked when they were only a few miles from Augusta. He hated to push, but who knew when they'd have a chance to talk in private again?

"I'm not brooding."

"Could have fooled me."

"Okay. I *am* brooding. Wouldn't you?"

There wasn't much he could say to that. He supposed she'd been hoping that Miss Emily would offer some more acceptable explanation for the fact that her grandfather had lied to her.

"Come upstairs with me," Ariadne said as they pulled into the dooryard.

A quick glance at her face told Clay he wasn't being invited into the lady's boudoir. She appeared to be on the verge of tears again.

"Are you sure that's a good idea?" he asked.

"I have something to show you. A letter Gramps left for me with Miss Emily." Ariadne got out of the car and left him to follow her to her apartment.

Slowly Clay removed the keys from the ignition. Swallowing his doubts, he headed for the stairs. By the time he reached her living room, she'd slipped out of her coat and was curled up on one end of the sofa. She'd opened up the letter and was rereading it.

Clay left his jacket on and perched on the edge of one of her straight-backed chairs. "What does it say?"

"That he never told me the truth because he was trying to protect me. He sounds bitter. He blames my mother for everything. He says she seduced my father, and that she broke his heart. That she was the only one who wanted a divorce."

Clay caught himself just in time, before he blurted out that George Allandale claimed Mark Palmer had been paid to leave Phyllis alone. Clay believed Palmer had not only taken the bribe but demanded it, but he doubted Ariadne was ready to hear that allegation. The fact that George didn't want her to know about it yet was of secondary importance. Clay was reluctant to shatter any more of Ariadne's illusions than he had to.

"He also says that my father died in a motorcycle accident because he developed a reckless streak after his marriage failed." Ariadne sent an accusatory look his way. "Did you know that?"

"Yes, I did. It was included in Duncan's report." There had been a clipping, too, he remembered. "Your father wasn't wearing a helmet."

She didn't say anything, but he thought he could guess what she was thinking. Here was one more lie her grandfather had told. There had never been any car crash. Neither her mother nor her father had died the way she'd been told they had.

"May I see the letter?" Clay asked.

She handed it over without comment. Clay quickly scanned the brief missive. Added to what she'd already told him was Edward Palmer's bald statement that he'd hoped she'd never find out that she had a mother still living. He tried to justify his deceit, but he never really explained the reasoning behind it. Instead, he wrote assurances that he loved Ariadne and that he'd only been trying to do what he thought was best for her.

"His warning seems sincere." Clay surprised himself by trying to find excuses for Edward Palmer. "Perhaps he was just mistaken about Phyllis. It's possible that your father didn't tell your grandfather the whole story." It was even possible that Edward Palmer never knew his son had taken a bribe to agree to divorce Phyllis Allandale.

"You knew my mother. Could she have broken his heart? Was she some kind of femme fatale?"

"She was a very unhappy woman who didn't always know what she wanted." At least, that's what Clay's own mother always said. He'd never had much direct contact with Phyllis himself, though he'd certainly been aware of the negative effects her whirlwind visits and bursts of motherly enthusiasm, followed by long absences, had had on Fay.

Ariadne had more questions, questions Clay preferred to evade. "I'm not the one you should be asking," he insisted.

"I'd ask my grandfather, but he's dead." Ariadne's fingers made a nervous rustling in the pocket of her skirt.

"What have you got there?"

Almost defiantly, she produced another letter. "Gramps left a final message for Phaedra, too." When he reached for it, she stuffed it back into her pocket. "It's for Fay's eyes only. I'm not going to open it, and neither are you."

At least, he thought, she was starting to think of her twin as a real person. They were making progress. "How are you planning to get it to her?"

"I could mail it."

"Better to deliver it in person. That way you can answer her questions about your grandfather." Lowering himself onto the sofa beside her, he took one of her soft hands in his own. "We may never have the whole story. Or understand the reasoning behind the actions people took. But the only way you'll ever be able to sort everything out is to meet the rest of the family. Talk to them yourself. Let them help you fill in a few of the blanks.''

The confusion and distress in her eyes tore at him, though why he should care so much about the sensibilities of a woman he'd known less than a week was beyond his comprehension. He told himself that he was merely carrying out an assignment. He'd been sent here to persuade her to make contact with the Allandales. It was the right thing to do. What he'd told her was only good sense. She should go and judge for herself what they were like. The irony was that George Allandale was probably a bigger liar than Edward Palmer had ever been. George was prepared to go to any extremes necessary in order to protect Fay, the grandchild he had raised.

"Your grandfather apparently thought he had to lie in order to protect a small child from people he didn't trust," Clay said aloud.

"I have a child to protect, too," she whispered.

"How can meeting the Allandales harm Shanna?" He lifted her chin with one finger until she had to meet his steady gaze. "You'll be right there with her."

She looked shell-shocked again and his heart ached for her. He knew he ought to keep after her until she agreed to do what he wanted. Instead, what he wanted most was to cradle her in his arms and make the hurt go away.

"I'm scared, Clay."

"Of what? There's nothing to be afraid of. They just want to meet you. Who knows? Maybe you'll get lucky and they'll decide they don't want anything to do with you. You'll be off the hook."

That remark earned him a tentative smile. A pity he

was serious. George might very well decide to sever the relationship.

"It's change that frightens me," Ariadne admitted, responding to his earlier question. "Change isn't always good, you know. And it's hard to go back once you've made the wrong choice."

Was she thinking of Shanna? Something told Clay she'd never regretted having a baby, even if the circumstances surrounding the child's birth hadn't been ideal. The more he knew of Ariadne, the more he suspected that she'd had stars, not dollar signs, in her eyes when she'd gotten pregnant.

"I threw a lot at you, out of the blue." In spite of his resolution to keep distance between them, his arm slid around her shoulders. Her lips trembled, but she didn't look away.

Kissing her was not a good idea.

Clay leaned his head back against the high top of the sofa and broke eye contact. "We'll work this out," he promised. "I'll do all I can to make things easier."

"I know you will. Thank you, Clay."

She let herself sag against his chest. Temptation returned with a vengeance. Somehow, Clay's hand found its way into her hair and, one by one, the pins came loose until all those long, gently curling tendrils were freed from confinement. Only then did he look at her. He'd been right. She had beautiful hair.

"You should wear it loose all the time," he murmured.

He leaned toward her. Whisper soft, his lips brushed hers. Ariadne started to return the kiss. Her hands tightened on his shoulders. And then, as if she suddenly realized where this was leading, she pulled back.

Wide confused eyes stared at him, haunted by a

bleakness that effectively killed any amorous ideas he might still be harboring. She was desirable. He could make her willing. And they'd both regret it if they gave in to a moment of weakness.

"Damn," Clay muttered. "I'm sorry, Ari. I didn't mean for that to happen."

"Things are complicated enough."

"Believe me, I know that." And yet it still took all his willpower not to reach out and tuck that one wayward strand of dark hair back behind her ear.

"I don't know what I want to do," she whispered shakily. "About anything. I...need to think. I need some time alone."

"Your doubts are natural," he admitted.

He wasn't talking about the Allandales any longer. Just as he had, Ariadne had been fighting the attraction between them from the start. They hadn't shared much of a kiss just now, but it had been enough to reinforce his earlier conviction that he wasn't the only one who felt a flare of good old-fashioned lust every time they got within touching distance.

"I think you'd better go now." He thought he heard regret in her voice. "I have to go pick up Shanna."

"You're too shaky to be driving. Let me."

She surprised him by agreeing.

("Mary Sue Pritchard says everybody has a daddy," Shanna announced as soon as she was settled in the back seat of the car. "Do I have a daddy?"

"Great timing," Ariadne said under her breath. Then she turned as far as the shoulder harness would allow and smiled at her daughter. "Mary Sue is right, Shanna. Everyone has a daddy, but some daddys don't live with their little girls."

Clay could just see the top of Shanna's head in his rearview mirror. She was nodding solemnly in response to her mother's words.

"Mary Sue Pritchard spends every weekend with her daddy. She has an extra mommy, but she doesn't like the second one very much."

"About your daddy, Shanna. He... Well, he hasn't been around for a while, but just the other day he came to Aunt Laurie's to talk to me about you."

A slight adjustment in the rearview mirror allowed Clay to see Shanna's reaction. Her elfin features lit up at the thought that she had a father. Clay's hands clenched on the wheel. Brad Comfort didn't deserve a little girl like Shanna. She ought to have a father who was there for her, not an irresponsible cad who only showed an interest in her because his new wife had.

Clay glanced at the mirror again. This time Shanna's big brown eyes locked on his.

"Are *you* my daddy?" she asked.

Clay nearly ran up onto the curb. His every thought scrambled, and he slowed his speed to a crawl and kept his eyes glued on the road ahead. She was just a kid, he reminded himself. There was even a sort of logic in her question, given the way Ariadne had broached the subject of Brad's reappearance in their lives. He wished she'd say something to get him off the hook with her daughter, but she seemed as thunderstruck by Shanna's conclusion as he was.

"Are you?" the four-year-old repeated.

Clay swallowed hard and continued to avoid the rearview mirror. He didn't risk glancing toward the passenger seat, either, but there was no evading the question.

He tried to keep his voice gentle. He didn't want

Shanna to think he wouldn't want to be her father. To his own surprise, he didn't find the concept as appalling as he should have. He shrugged aside that insight to think about later. Much later.

"I'm not your father, Shanna. But if I were, I'd be very happy to have a little girl like you."

Finding her voice at last, Ariadne tried to clarify the situation. "Your daddy has a new wife, just like Mary Sue Pritchard's daddy."

Shanna said nothing to that. She was waiting until she snagged Clay's gaze again. The moment he glanced at her in the mirror, she sent him a heart-melting smile and made him an offer that left him speechless.

"You can be my extra daddy if you want," she said.

Chapter Five

Although she was bundled up against the cold, Ariadne still shivered. When the icy wind cut through her heavy coat and warm boots, it chilled her all the way to the bone. Another sort of coldness came from being here at her grandfather's grave.

It had all happened so suddenly, she thought, staring at the monolithic marker with PALMER carved deep into the granite. Gramps had had a heart attack. There had been no warning at all. One day he'd been hale and hearty as ever. The next day he'd been dead.

Once Ariadne's faith in her grandfather, her certainty about who she was, had been just as solid as the monument in this family plot. Now the memorial mocked her, making her wonder if she'd ever succeed in her quest for peace of mind.

Coming here was not the most rational thing she'd ever done, but Ariadne had been unable to think of any other way to communicate with her grandfather. She only wished she could really talk to him one last time, to set things right between them.

Then she might be able to get on with her life.

"Gramps," she began in a whisper, "I think I understand what you did when I was three. And I think you deliberately left the photograph for me to find, just as you left that letter with Miss Emily. That was the right thing to do, too, but I can't help wishing that you'd told me yourself. I wish there had been time for me to ask you questions. It's…hard finding out this way. And this other family…I don't know how I feel about them."

She was curious about Fay, and bothered by the fact that Clay evaded so many of the questions she asked about her sister. Ariadne knew little more than that Fay lived in Hartford, was separated from her husband and worked freelance for a public relations firm. "Wait until you meet her for yourself," Clay kept saying. The suggestion always made perfect sense and yet, at the same time, on each occasion that he put her off with those words, she was left with a vague sense of uneasiness. She couldn't help feeling that there was something significant he wasn't telling her.

Ariadne sighed deeply. She'd find out all about Fay soon enough. First, though, she had to prepare Shanna for the fact that she had a set of great-grandparents and an aunt. She wasn't sure how her daughter would deal with a stranger in that special relationship of great-grandfather. Ariadne grimaced. She wasn't sure how she would herself. After all, she'd already had the best grandfather in the world.

Even if he *had* lied to her all her life.

"I wish I'd been able to meet my mother," she said aloud. "I'd have liked to get to know her."

Taking a deep breath, she stared down at the plot. It was covered with snow now, and there was no sign left of the single rose she'd left on the newly turned earth after the funeral. "Your letter said that you wanted to protect me by keeping me from my mother, but you never really explained why. I don't have any convincing reasons to stay away from her family."

Disappointment nagged at her. His concept of leaving an account of his side of the story was far different from her own. She'd gone to Miss Emily hoping to learn the real reason behind the lies. She had come away with only part of the story. His letter had raised more questions than it had answered. Vague allegations implying that none of the Allandales were fit to raise a child, but not saying why, were not helpful.

"My mother couldn't have been too awful, could she?" Ariadne whispered. "I mean, my father let her keep Fay."

She didn't want to dwell on the possibility that her sister had been mistreated in some way. Clay hadn't given her any indication of that, though he did, at times, seem awfully protective in his attitude toward her twin.

Frowning, she focused her thoughts on Gramps again. There would be time later to deal with her mixed feelings about Clay Franklin. Her second sigh sounded loud in the deserted cemetery. "You meant well. I do believe that."

A single tear slid down her cheek and plopped onto the frozen surface. The last few days had been filled with restless nights, troubling dreams and roller-coaster emotions, but the thinking she'd been forced to do had led her to one inescapable conclusion.

She was suddenly glad she'd come to the cemetery. The act had cleared the air somehow, and confirmed her decision. When she spoke again, her words were from the heart. "I love you, Gramps," she whispered. "And I forgive you."

When she finally turned away from the grave, the mind-numbing indecision that had been plaguing her was gone. The uncomfortable feeling that had haunted her since Clay first convinced her he was telling the truth, the sense that she didn't know for certain who she was anymore, continued to nag at her, but at least now she knew exactly what she had to do in order to find out.

Crunching through the snow, she made her way out of the cemetery. The only other sound was the distant hum of traffic and yet, before she'd gone more than a few yards, she knew she was no longer alone.

Clay was waiting for her just outside the gate.

"Why am I not surprised?" she muttered under her breath.

"Laurie told me you'd come here," he said. "I don't mean to intrude, but I thought you might like some company on the walk home."

Her glance flicked upward to the clear blue winter sky. "I've been here longer than I realized. It must be well past noon."

"Did the long walk and the fresh air help?"

She liked walking in the fall, he remembered, just as he did. This close to her, though, his thoughts jumped instead to other seasons. Her delicate perfume, summer, mingled with a hint of pine from surrounding trees, and the distinctive winter odor of wool made wet by snow.

"I'm ready to meet the rest of my family now," she announced as they headed back. "At least, I'm as ready as I'll ever be."

"Good."

"You sound relieved," she remarked. "Tired of bird-dogging me?"

A weak smile was the only answer he could manage to her teasing remark. She'd accurately read his reaction, but not the reason behind it. He knew he ought to have been bored to tears this past week, champing at the bit to get back to Connecticut. Instead, he'd developed an inexplicable and insidious longing to chuck it all, to stay right here until he got tired of Ariadne's company.

"I'll need to make arrangements with Laurie," she said. "I suppose I can take up to a week off, but—"

"I've already talked to Laurie. She said she can manage alone for two."

"One." Her voice was so sharp that his steps faltered.

He slanted a look at her face and realized she was seriously annoyed. "Problem?"

"There are things I admire about you, Clay, but this tendency to take charge is not one of them. I prefer to make my own plans."

The chilly breeze ruffled her hair and turned her cheeks a bright, healthy color. The flash of irritation in her dark eyes only made her more appealing. Clay silently cursed the circumstances that obliged him to keep his hands to himself.

"Then you probably won't be happy about this, either." Clay reached into the inside pocket of his overcoat and pulled out a packet with an airline logo emblazoned on the outside. Inside were tickets for a direct flight from Portland to Tampa—leaving the next day in the afternoon.

After Ariadne inspected the contents of the packet, she said nothing. They started walking again, until she came to a stop in front of Frounfelker's Antiques. She pretended an interest in the window display while she tried to decide how to deal with her mixed feelings about what Clay had done.

She could sense his uneasiness as he stood next to her, close but not quite touching. She had to stiffen her spine in order not to sway toward him. He drew her like a magnet, daring her to defy all common sense.

Reflected in the plate-glass window, they were not quite touching, not quite communicating, but almost. Clay's image slanted a worried look in her direction. "Better to get it over with," he said reasonably. "You know you'll have to make the trip sometime."

"Yes," she agreed.

It was just that at this moment the trip—even the prospect of meeting her family—took a back seat to thoughts of Clay Franklin. She was dreaming if she thought a relationship between them would ever work. Dreams were just the problem, too. She'd had a doozy about him the previous night.

The breeze was welcome, cooling her flaming cheeks as she began to walk again. They were only two blocks from the bookstore and her apartment. She didn't know whether to wish they were closer, or on the other side of the continent. Once Clay had delivered her into the hands of her family, she might never see him again.

While she regretted the loss of what might have

been, Ariadne told herself firmly that she'd probably read too much into his attentions these past few days. That was all part of his job. She drew in a deep breath of crisp, reviving air and reminded herself that she'd made a few tentative plans of her own while she was in the cemetery.

"There are two things I need to do before I meet the Allandales," she told Clay. "First, I have to prepare Shanna. Explain that we're going to see family. And that she has an aunt who looks just like Mommy. I'll talk to her tonight."

Risking a glance at Clay, she saw that his expression was closed, completely unrevealing.

"The second thing is that I want to change the flight so we can stop in Hartford on our way south. I want to meet my sister without our grandparents there."

Tension radiated from him with almost palpable force. Ariadne felt a moment's panic as she waited for him to speak. Was there something he hadn't told her? Some reason for going directly to Florida?

But his reply contained no hint of the turmoil she'd sensed earlier. His voice was…polite. "I'll call the airline. Tomorrow all right if there are seats available?"

"Yes, that's fine," she blurted. "Tomorrow."

Ariadne hoped she hadn't just made the biggest mistake of her life. Not about going to visit the Allandales. She had no choice there. This family thing had to be settled. But her budding relationship with Clay seemed to be inextricably tied in to the trip. She wondered if she'd just closed off any possibility of a relationship with him…before that door had even been opened halfway.

The next twenty-four hours passed in a blur. Clay got them to the airport and onto a plane. All Ariadne had to do was pack for herself and Shanna and keep the little girl occupied on the long trip. That was enough. She didn't have time to worry about what her sister would be like until they were getting off the plane in Hartford.

What if she didn't like this twin sister of hers? What if they had absolutely nothing in common?

"This way to Baggage Claim," Clay said, taking her arm to steer her in the right direction.

Numbly, Ariadne went.

Where was Fay? Hadn't she come to meet their plane, after all?

"Look, Mommy," Shanna whispered.

Ariadne looked.

There was no doubt in her mind about the identity of the tall, dark-haired woman coming toward them. And at least one of Ariadne's questions was immediately answered. Ariadne had worn comfortable wool slacks for the trip—pale gray ones with decent-size pockets. She'd added a patterned sweater, mostly blue and gray, and a strand of blue beads.

Except for the beads, Fay was dressed in almost exactly the same way. The pattern of her sweater was different, adding a pale green to the blue and gray, and her gray slacks had no pockets, making her appear a bit slimmer than her twin, but otherwise they looked as if they'd purposely coordinated their outfits.

Ariadne should have felt reassured, but in truth she was shaken by the coincidence. With awkward steps she moved forward. She'd already accepted, intellectually, that Clay's story was true, that she had an identical twin sister, but being here, seeing her in person, was an unexpectedly emotional experience. She felt as

if she'd been punched in the stomach and was having
a little trouble catching her breath.

She had a twin. An identical twin.

"Mind-boggling, isn't it?" Fay asked. Her mouth
kicked up at one corner and her eyes invited Ariadne
to share in the absurdity of their situation.

A moment later they were hugging each other, overflowing with tears and with a helpless laughter that left
them both weak.

"You're in a heap of trouble, boss." Clay's secretary, Nancy Kelly, held out a handful of pink message
slips. From the sympathetic expression on her face, she
was only half kidding.

"Let me guess. They're all from George Allandale."

"You got it."

Grimly, Clay reached for the offensive little pieces
of paper, tightened his fist around the lot and headed
for the privacy of the inner office, already regretting
his decision to come in for a few hours. It was after
four. He could have stayed at home when Fay dropped
him off. Better yet, he could have been more persuasive
about accompanying the twins to Fay's place. When
he'd offered to take them all out to dinner, Fay'd stuck
her tongue out at him, the brat, and told him to go
away. Feeling like a third wheel on a ten-speed bike,
he'd let her drive away, taking Ari and Shanna with
her.

All the messages were the same. "Call at once. What
the hell is going on?"

"I wish I knew," Clay muttered as he punched in
George's Florida number.

Seeing the twins together had confirmed what Clay
had suspected the moment he walked into Ariadne's

bookstore. There had never been and still wasn't any spark between himself and Fay. They had nothing but plain old friendship between them. But all Ari had to do was touch his hand to ask if he had the baggage claim checks and he felt a jolt of desire so strong it was all he could do not to pull her into his arms and kiss her senseless.

Whatever this was that he felt for Ariadne Palmer kept getting stronger. It was far more powerful than simple lust. Unlike anything he'd ever felt for any woman. He balked at giving it a name.

"You were supposed to bring her directly to me," George Allandale bellowed as soon as he came on the line. "Why in God's name did you have to stop in Hartford?"

"That was her condition, George. Meet her twin sister first or she didn't leave Maine at all."

Clay resented George's unrelenting prejudice against Ari as much as he'd always disliked the man's attempts to control Fay's decisions, but he'd learned over the years that losing his temper served no useful purpose and usually just made matters worse. That was especially true in dealing with powerful, stubborn men like George Allandale.

As the tirade of accusations and complaints continued, Clay had to remind himself again and again that while it might feel good for a moment to tell George off, yielding to impulse would have dire consequences. He doubted that Franklin, Manley, Murphy, Franklin and Teasdale would lose George Allandale as a client, but quarreling with the old man could adversely affect Clay's ability to help Fay through this particularly rough patch in her life.

Wait it out, he warned himself. At least part of

George's anger was pure bluster. He didn't like it that he wasn't the one in control. Clay knew George did genuinely care about Fay's well-being. He just went about looking out for her best interests in a domineering, high-handed, even manipulative manner. He was skilled at provoking feelings of guilt, too.

By the time George finally wound down, Clay's tie was undone and a dozen paper clips had been twisted into unrecognizable shapes and scattered across the pristine green blotter that rested exactly at the center of his oak desk.

"Have a little faith in your granddaughter, George," Clay suggested when he could get a word in. He didn't specify which one.

"What happened at the airport? What did they say to each other?"

In spite of his irritation at George, a small smile tugged at the corners of Clay's mouth as he recounted their meeting. "They're a lot alike," he said when he'd summarized that first encounter.

"Hardly. Fay'd never have a child out of wedlock."

Clay wondered. He'd seen the longing in Fay's gaze when she'd first set eyes on Shanna. It was certainly true, though, that Shanna was one of the biggest differences between the twins. His smile widened as he saw the scene at the airport in his mind's eye.

Shanna, suddenly overcome by shyness and confusion, had tugged at the bottom of her mother's sweater and then, when Ari turned, had locked her arms around Ari's thighs. Even when Fay knelt down, so that she was eye to eye with Shanna, the little girl wouldn't release Mommy and say hello to Aunt Fay. Instead, Shanna had buried her face in the soft wool of Ari's slacks and refused to look at anyone. With her daughter still clinging to her legs, making it difficult for Ari to walk, they'd claimed their baggage and headed for the parking lot.

"Reserve judgment, George," Clay advised. He put the conversation on the speaker phone and stood up to stretch. "Everything I've seen of her tells me that Ariadne Palmer is a very honest, hardworking woman. And a good mother."

"That's what she *appears* to be."

"She objected to the expense of first-class airplane tickets on the grounds that they're a wasteful extravagance. Does that sound like someone who's out for all she can get?"

"A clever ploy."

Clay frowned at the speaker, shaking his head. "Only if she already knows how wealthy you are, and I don't believe she does. To tell you the truth, George, I think she might be even more reluctant to visit if she knew you had money. She hasn't had very good experiences with rich men."

"Couldn't get one to marry her, you mean. Of course she'd be bitter about that."

"She's not a gold digger, but I don't suppose you'll take my word for it. You'll see for yourself tomorrow. The flight lands in Tampa around one. Will you meet the plane or should I rent a car?"

George had a strategy all mapped out. Clay only had to listen and agree, but he couldn't stop himself from making one last attempt to dissuade Fay and Ari's grandfather from his plans.

"You'll find she puts a high premium on honesty, George. All this deceit is unnecessary, and it may well backfire. What if you alienate your granddaughter so completely that she wants nothing more to do with you?''

But George wasn't listening. He rarely did when someone said something he didn't want to hear. "What's happened to your common sense, Clayton?" he grumbled irritably. "I'm disappointed in you."

He disconnected without waiting for a response, and without giving Clay a chance to correct his mistaken impression that Fay planned to stay behind when Clay and Ariadne flew out of Hartford tomorrow.

Common sense?

With a sound of disgust, Clay pushed a button to hang up on his end. Jerking his tie off completely, he flung it into the plush visitor's chair on the opposite side of his desk.

George didn't mean common sense. He didn't want common sense. He'd been relying on one of Clay's far less admirable traits. George had been counting on Clay's cynicism to keep him from giving Ariadne Palmer credit for any honesty at all.

Clay stopped in front of the plate-glass window and stared unseeing at the bustle of Hartford's business district far below. The terrible truth was that with anyone but Ariadne Palmer, Clay's innate distrust of people would have kept him objective. He'd have believed the worst, suspected her of lying until it was proven otherwise, and remained aloof. Cold. Unfeeling.

When had it happened? When had he become so inured to the worst in human nature that he'd stopped believing anyone but a few old friends were trustworthy?

Skepticism was good. Cynicism was another matter entirely. Somehow, slowly, insidiously, over five solid years of handling one nasty divorce case after another, he'd slipped over the line. That realization was difficult enough to deal with on its own, but what shook Clay even more deeply was his acknowledgment that the reason he could now step outside of himself and see what he had become was Ariadne Palmer.

Until he'd met Ari, he'd rarely taken the time to assess his life-style, his career or his increasingly cynical attitude toward women, marriage and family. A few hours with her had shaken him out of his preconceived notions. She'd made him want to believe in her. More than that, she'd made him want to believe in happy endings.

Had she manipulated him?

Irritated, Clay turned away from the window and stalked back to his desk. Stacks of file folders were neatly piled there—all the cases needing his attention. For a moment he regarded them with extreme distaste, tempted to ignore them, to go back to Fay's and find out what was happening. To spend more time with the most enigmatic, fascinating woman he'd ever met and the little girl who'd told him he could be her "extra daddy."

Nancy buzzed him. "Your father would like a word with you," she said when he picked up.

First George Allandale. Now Clayton Franklin Sr. He definitely should not have come into the office.

"Has he had a call from Florida in the last five minutes?" Clay asked his secretary.

"No, sir. And he came in after you arrived." She lowered her voice. "I think he's upset about something."

Great. That was all he needed.

But Clay dutifully made his way to his father's office.

In looks they were very similar. Clayton senior was as physically fit as his son. Only the distinguished gray in his hair gave away his age. Nancy had been right. He did look worried about something. Clay didn't have to search far for the probable cause of his father's anxiety. Her picture was right there on his desk.

Barbara Teasdale Franklin. Clay's stepmother. Full partner in Franklin, Manley, Murphy, Franklin and Teasdale.

And the only woman Clay himself had ever asked to marry him.

A familiar bitterness seeped into Clay's soul. He'd thought he was in love with Barbara. Her only love was for herself. Thank God he'd balked at signing the prenuptial agreement she'd handed him. He was all for potential marriage partners protecting themselves, but that damn thing had been an insult. It had even specified what would happen to their hypothetical children when he and Barbara divorced.

When, not if.

And the real price tag hadn't even been the wedding ring. Barbara had demanded a partnership in the family firm. He'd never dreamed, when he broke it off with her, that she'd turn right around and marry his father instead. Then again, he'd never dreamed, as a child growing up in what he'd thought of as a perfect, happy home, that his parents would ever split up. They'd divorced a few years after he'd left the nest. Apparently, he'd been the only thing they had in common, the only reason they'd stayed together as long as they had.

Barbara hadn't played any part in ending his parents' marriage. That was the only thing that made her continued presence in the law offices tolerable. But she had taken advantage of his father's vulnerability after the divorce. She'd easily substituted one Franklin for the other and married his dad in Las Vegas a month to the day after Clay refused to sign away his unborn children's future.

Clay supposed he ought to feel a sense of smug superiority now that it looked as if Barbara had begun to make his father's life a living hell, but he was denied even that satisfaction. He hated seeing what she'd done to the older man. He wanted to help if he could.

"Do you want to talk about it, Dad?" he asked. "I'm told I'm a good listener."

Chapter Six

Overwhelmed.

That was the only word for how she felt. Nothing
had prepared Ariadne for the stunning impact of having
so many similarities with Fay interspersed with jarring
little differences.

After that first hug at the airport, new insecurities
had immediately set in. She'd grown increasingly nervous during the drive to her sister's apartment, especially after they dropped Clay off, even when Fay
swung the car in at the drive-up window of a popular
burger chain and Shanna abruptly recovered from her
bout of shyness.

Three hours later, Ariadne sat at her twin sister's
breakfast bar finishing a cup of after-supper hot cocoa
and watching the two of them. It was a bit disconcerting, like seeing a reflection of herself, but she was beginning to get used to it.

She glanced at the kitchen clock. "Bedtime, Shanna."

"No, it's not."

"Yes, it is, pumpkin. We've got another long, busy day ahead of us tomorrow."

Shanna fussed, but eventually was persuaded to cooperate, if she could take Aunt Fay's teddy bear to bed with her. She'd discovered the handmade teddy sitting in a special bear-size chair on a small corner table in the living room.

"Fay, she's only four. If that's worth a lot of—"

"Her smile is worth far more."

Unable to doubt her sister's sincerity, Ariadne swallowed her warning. Shanna was careful of her toys, but this bear had never been intended to be one. Valuable books were Ariadne's field of expertise, not designer teddy bears, but she knew something of their value from all the antique and collectible shows she'd attended. At a guess, Teddy had cost at least $500.

Ariadne was glad her twin didn't have to worry about money, but she was a little uncomfortable with the fact that everything Fay owned was expensive. Luxurious touches were everywhere—understated but obvious. Their impact had been lessened, however, when she'd walked into Fay's guest room and spotted eight framed, late-nineteenth-century fashion prints. Three matched those that hung in Ariadne's bedroom back in Maine. For all that they'd been raised apart, and in vastly different circumstances, it seemed that she and her twin had some tastes in common.

"Clay wouldn't say much about you," Ariadne remarked after they'd settled Shanna for the night and returned to Fay's spacious living room.

"Clay can be frustratingly closemouthed," Fay

agreed. "I suppose that makes him a good lawyer. That and the fact that he's so easy to talk to."

"He kept telling me I should wait until I met you and ask you all my questions."

Wearily pulling pins out of her hair, running her fingers through the long, thick locks, Ariadne paused, suddenly assaulted by the clear memory of Clay performing the same task. A wave of sensual longing momentarily swamped her. She repressed it, but not without considerable effort.

Fay settled in at the opposite end of the living room sofa, facing her twin. "It's like looking into a mirror, except that you make me wish I hadn't cut my hair."

"Did you ever suspect I existed? When you were growing up, I mean."

"No. If twins are supposed to have some psychic link, I guess ours got severed when we were separated."

Ariadne didn't know any easy way to begin, but Fay understood when she blurted out the first bald questions. "Why did she wait so long to tell you? Didn't our mother want to know what happened to me?"

"I don't know. I wish I did."

"Didn't you ask?"

"She was in the hospital." Fay couldn't conceal her shudder. "I hate hospitals. I know I should have stayed right at her bedside, but I couldn't. And part of the time, it just seemed like she was raving."

Feeling her sister's anguish, Ariadne reached out. They clasped hands. Somehow that helped. After a moment, Fay was able to continue.

"Mother traveled a lot. She left me with her parents and did adventurous things like joining archaeological digs and going treasure hunting. She spent six months once in the jungles of South America.''

Amazed, Ariadne couldn't think of a single response to make to that revelation. She waited for Fay to continue.

''She picked up an exotic illness or two along the way. For the last couple of years, Mother was in and out of the hospital a lot. Then, when she had to have what should have been a routine gallbladder removal, everything that could go wrong, did. She had some kind of reaction to the medication. It made her... well...almost psychotic for a while.''

As Fay described an episode during which their mother had been convinced that the nurses had stolen her designer sunglasses, Ariadne had the oddest sensation that she'd been there in the hospital with her twin. She could sense Fay's distaste for her surroundings, her uneasiness at the way their mother's ravings were so casually dismissed. Ariadne could almost smell the disinfectant, the unappetizing aroma of hospital food, the distinctive and lingering scent that permeated the sweat of a person on drugs. For an instant she even heard the beep of monitors, and the low hum of voices. One belonged to her mother and it was well launched into a litany of petty complaints and irrational claims.

Ariadne shook her head to clear away the confusion of images. Her imagination was working overtime. It must be, because her only personal experience with hospitals had been when Shanna was born, and even then she'd only been in a pretty, nonthreatening birthing room. She had been spared long hours at Gramps's bedside. He'd died at the bowling alley, halfway through a tournament and surrounded by his friends.

''So, she had new glasses made and the hospital paid

for them," Fay said, wrapping up the anecdote. "About six months after that the doctors discovered that one of those infections she'd had in the jungle had damaged her heart. They replaced a valve, but something was wrong with it. She was in for the second operation when she told me about you. All of a sudden, one day when she'd been having bad spells interspersed with lucid moments because of all the drugs they were giving her, she suddenly stared right at me and said, 'Find your sister.'"

Fay tried to smile but didn't quite manage it. "It was so strange, Ari. I should have dismissed it as the medicine talking. I mean, earlier that day she'd been raving about getting the dog out of the road, and she didn't even own a dog. But somehow I knew. And the next day, when she seemed to be recovering and almost herself again, I tried to pin her down."

"Tried?"

Fay nodded. "Succeeded, but only to an extent. At first she denied it. And even when she finally told me the truth, there were so many questions I didn't think to ask. I thought there would be time."

Giving her sister a moment to recover herself, Ariadne tried to imagine what she'd have felt if, before he died, Gramps had had time to tell her that she had a sister. Would she have believed him? It might have been tempting to dismiss the whole episode as a drug-induced hallucination.

The doorbell rang just as Fay reached for a tissue to blot her moist eyes. She carried it with her to the foyer. Ariadne heard her murmur something, and then Clay's voice asked, "What's wrong, babe? You look like you've been crying."

Phaedra's answer was too softly spoken for Ariadne

to hear, but a moment later, when the two of them entered the living room arm in arm, she looked much more cheerful. Ariadne's smile of greeting was forced and something of her irritation at the interruption must have shown through. Clay gave her a hard look before he turned to address her twin.

"I won't stay long," he promised. "I just wanted to make sure you knew when I'd be picking all of you up tomorrow for the airport."

"Fay was telling me about our mother," Ariadne said pointedly. She refrained from asking why he hadn't just phoned to confirm the arrangements. Truthfully, she didn't know how she felt about his arrival, or if she wanted him to go or stay. She did wish he'd release his hold on her sister.

"Coffee?" Fay asked. "Cocoa? There's still some on the stove."

"I can help myself."

As soon as he headed for the kitchen, Fay perched nervously on the edge of a chair. "I was telling you about the questions I asked Mother. She admitted that when she and our father divorced they agreed to each take one of us." Fay shook her head in disbelief. "She laughed, Ari. She said they stole the idea from an old Disney movie, *The Parent Trap*. I guess we were supposed to meet somehow as teenagers and scheme to get our parents back together, the way the twins did in that story. Only, it didn't work out that way. Mother never really explained why she didn't try to find him again, but I got the impression that she didn't know he was dead. She talked as if he deliberately disappeared, thwarting her plans to reunite us."

"Didn't her parents know where he was? Surely

they must have known something about the man she married.''

"They didn't want to know." Fay sounded bitter. "They cut her out of their lives entirely until she dumped me on their doorstep. They certainly didn't want anything to do with him."

Him. Mark Palmer. Ariadne's father.

Unable to sit still any longer, Fay left her chair and began to pace. Clay came back into the room, a cup of cocoa in one hand. His worried gaze followed Fay's restless movements.

"I should have stayed right there at the hospital," she said, "but I couldn't stand it. I left for the night. I thought we'd have years to sort things out."

"What happened?"

"The phone system killed her," Fay blurted.

"What?"

"I'm sorry. Give me a minute." She gripped the bookshelves, head bowed, and took several deep breaths.

Clay crossed quickly to her side and handed her the cocoa. When she'd taken a couple of sips and put the cup down, he stayed where he was, taking her hand in his and giving it a comforting squeeze. Ariadne looked away, feeling as if she'd been spying on a private moment.

"I never said that out loud before," Fay admitted, "but when they called me to say she was dead, that's what I thought. The last memory I have of her is just so…absurd."

Confused, Ariadne let her sister gather herself together. She was getting a disjointed picture of their mother and beginning to wonder if anything about this new family of hers would be simple and straightforward.

"It had become something we joked about," Fay said. Shaking Clay off, she returned to the sofa, once more settling in next to her twin. "Every time she was in the hospital, she'd have all kinds of trouble using the phone. It probably had to do with the medication. Again. Her movements were clumsy and she'd cut herself off. Anyway, when I called her that last night, to tell her I'd be in first thing in the morning to visit her, it happened again. She thought we'd been completely disconnected, although I was actually still on the line. I decided I'd let it ride. After all, I was sure I'd see her again in just a few hours."

A sound that was somewhere between a sob and a laugh choked Fay. "That's the last memory I'll ever have of Mother. She was yelling for the nurse, telling her to fix the damn phone."

"You couldn't have known," Ariadne said.

"Ari's right," Clay agreed. "Don't torment yourself over it."

Fay shot grateful looks at each of them in turn. "I'm amazed sometimes by how much I miss her," she confessed. "We nearly always quarreled when we were together, but there's such a gap now. I find myself starting to pick up the phone to call and tell her the good news when one of my clients loves a new ad campaign I've designed for him. And then I remember she's gone. And that she left things in an awful muddle."

"I wish I'd had a chance to meet her," Ariadne said.

"She would have nagged you, too," Clay muttered.

The comment brought a hint of genuine amusement to Fay's expression. "You've got that right. She wouldn't have liked it that both of her daughters had failed relationships.''

Startled, Ariadne met her sister's eyes. Fay hadn't said much about Gary Vandemann, the husband from whom she was separated. Ariadne hesitated to ask. There were enough spooky parallels in their lives already. She wasn't sure she wanted to risk finding out that Gary was another Brad Comfort.

"You wish you'd known Mother," Fay said, "and I wish I'd known Grandfather Palmer."

Ariadne sensed a sudden tension in Clay. "Have you given her the letter yet?" he demanded.

"You needn't sound as if you think I meant to hide it," Ariadne told him. She'd wanted to get to know Fay a little better first, to judge how she'd react to receiving a message from beyond the grave. A glance at her twin told her she didn't have to worry, or explain why she'd delayed. Not to Fay. She reached into her purse, which she'd left next to the coffee table, and withdrew the folded envelope with "Phaedra" scrawled across the front in Gramps's familiar handwriting.

"I wish I'd known my grandfather Palmer," Fay repeated after she'd finished reading the short missive. "He sounds like a warm, loving man."

"He was. His only failing was in lying to me about my mother. He let me think I was alone in the world except for him. He seemed to believe he had to protect me from my mother and her parents, but they don't sound like ogres when you talk about them."

"No. They aren't, though Lord knows Mother wasn't the easiest person to get along with." Fay hesitated, then posed another question. "Are you angry with him? I was angry with Mother. For weeks. Angry that she'd separated us. Angry that she'd died. Just…angry.''

"I guess I was." Ariadne thought back to her visit to the cemetery. Had it only been yesterday? "I've been able to accept that his motives were good, even if his decisions did cost me the chance to know my mother. I really do forgive him. I loved him very much. That makes it easier.''

The phone rang. Fay's answering machine picked up and Ariadne heard a long silence after the beep and then the loud click of a person at the other end hanging up in frustration.

"That's the fifth time that's happened since I got here," she said, her gaze traveling from the phone to Fay to Clay.

"Are you being harassed?" he demanded, turning to his childhood friend.

"You could say that."

"Gary?"

Fay sighed. "No. That was Poppa on the phone. Sometimes it's easier to ignore him."

Shocked, Ariadne protested. "But what if it's an emergency? They're elderly. They—''

"If it was something like that, he'd have left a message," Clay said.

Ariadne's twin was nodding. "He wants to talk to me about you," she said bluntly, "but he doesn't want to say anything you might overhear.''

"I don't understand."

"I know you don't and I wish I could explain, but I can't.''

"Are you afraid of your grandfather?"

"Afraid? No. Never. Frustrated by. Annoyed with. He has a…forceful personality.'' She chuckled and exchanged a glance with Clay before she grinned at her sister. "Clay and I used to call him the General behind his back when we were kids."

"He tries to run the whole show," Clay said. "Most of the time it's simpler to let him, but this time, I think, someone should tell him he's out of line." He reached for his coat. "You two don't need me around this evening, anyway. Why don't I go home and give George a call and remind him we'll see him tomorrow? Suggest he curb his impatience to talk to you?"

"Good idea. Thanks, Clay. You're a doll."

While her sister saw him out, Ariadne pondered the connection between them. They'd seemed, more than once, to be exchanging messages with eyes and body language, messages she was not supposed to intercept, let alone interpret. Just old friends? She wondered. They knew each other well enough to all but finish one another's sentences.

"Well, that should spike the General's guns," Fay said as she plopped down on her end of the sofa once more.

"Was he in the military?"

"Oh, no. He's a retired businessman. He just acts like he's used to commanding troops."

A puzzled frown knit Ariadne's brow. She opened her mouth to inquire further about Allandale's background, but Fay stayed her by lifting both hands palms out.

"Look, Ari, I'd like to answer all your questions about him, but I promised him I wouldn't. He's got this thing about people talking about him behind his back." She hesitated, as if she wanted to elaborate, then shrugged and smiled a bit sheepishly. "He wanted to be present when we first met, you know. So I've already gone against his wishes by having you here."

For a moment, an infinite sadness clouded the features so like Ariadne's own. Then, with disconcerting swiftness, Fay turned the tables and shot a question of her own at Ariadne. "What did you do to him, anyway?"

"Your grandfather?" Ariadne asked in confusion.

"Not Poppa. Clay. He's not the same since his jaunt to Maine. I can't quite put my finger on the difference, but something has definitely changed."

"I didn't do anything to him, except maybe object when he tried to boss me around."

"Good for you."

Ariadne stared at her, wishing she understood what was behind her sister's obvious glee. "He told me that you two have been close friends ever since you were children," she said cautiously.

"That's true. We were almost more. Did he happen to mention that his parents and my—*our* grandparents tried to arrange a marriage between us?"

Taken aback, Ariadne didn't know what to say to that.

A faraway expression on her face, Fay was silent, too. Then she sent a sad smile in Ariadne's direction. "We politely declined their suggestion, of course. Sometimes I wonder if we made the right decision. On the other hand, it would hardly have been fair to marry my best friend unless I loved him, too."

"Did you love your husband?"

"I thought I did. And I thought he loved me. I ought to love him. He's charming, well educated, handsome. Rich, too." She gave Ariadne an odd look. "You'd think that would help."

"I'd think it would get in the way."

Fay lifted one eyebrow. "Oh? What's wrong with having money?"

"Nothing, I suppose, but after my experience with Shanna's father, I'm wary of rich men. They tend to be selfish, and self-centered. And they have some odd ideas about what's most important in life."

"Well, that certainly sums up a few of Gary's faults, but Clay doesn't fit the pattern, and you've probably figured out by now that he's not exactly struggling to make ends meet."

"I'm not interested in Clay in any romantic way."

The denial was automatic, but it was also a lie. Ariadne was appalled at how easy it had been to utter the words. Could one inherit a tendency to lie? she wondered.

A glance at her sister's face told Ariadne that she hadn't even lied well. Fay had seen right through the prevarication.

"Right." She sounded as skeptical as she looked.

"Romantic interest isn't enough," Ariadne defended herself. "Neither is physical attraction. There are just too many obstacles. We aren't at all suited to each other."

"Do go on," Fay teased. "This is fascinating."

Ariadne glared at her. "Our life-styles are completely different for one thing. Even if he wasn't well-off, we'd still be from entirely different worlds. I'd never fit into his. I can't pretend to be something I'm not." A short, rueful bark of humorless laughter escaped her. "I learned that from Brad, Shanna's father. If I'd had any sense, I'd have caught on the very first time I went out with him."

"Why? What happened?"

To her own surprise, Ariadne wanted to tell her. "I haven't thought about this in years," she admitted. Yet somehow it felt right to share the story with her sister. The longer she talked to Fay, the more it seemed as if they'd known each other all their lives.

"Brad and I met in college. After a few casual lunches in the campus snack bar, he invited me out for dinner. He took me to a ritzy French restaurant."

She still remembered how she'd felt when they'd walked into that place and been greeted by an effusive maitre d'. They'd been shown to a table draped in damask and decorated with freshly cut flowers. The delicate scent of the roses had been joined by the mouthwatering aromas of a dozen exotic dishes. Ariadne had realized, passing by other diners, that she didn't recognize any of the people or any of the things they were eating, but she'd still had the jaunty confidence of youth, bolstered by the fact that she was wearing the most expensive dress she'd ever owned, a soft jersey knit that clung to every curve. She'd bought it that same morning, just for this occasion, and would be eating peanut butter and jelly sandwiches for lunch and supper for the next month to make up for the extravagance.

"The whole evening should have been wonderfully romantic," Ariadne told her sister.

"And it wasn't?"

"It turned out that I wasn't as sophisticated as I thought I was, and certainly no match for Brad. He ordered Coquilles Saint-Jacques. I'd never heard them called that before. To me they were just sea scallops in a really great sauce, which is what I blurted right out. I have never been much good at thinking before I speak. My thoughts tend to go directly from brain to mouth. No internal censorship whatsoever.''

"That's not a bad characteristic," Fay said. "I wish more people were up-front and honest."

"You wouldn't think so if you'd heard me make a fool of myself over the sorbet. It looked like sherbet to me, and I promptly told the waiter I hadn't ordered dessert yet. After all, it was the middle of the meal. Brad didn't say a word, but the waiter, who had one of those snooty, carrying voices, informed me that sorbet was intended to cleanse the palate for the next course. I'd never heard such pretentious nonsense in my life and naturally I said so.''

"To the waiter?"

"No!" Ariadne laughed in spite of the painfulness the memory still held for her. "Even at twenty I wasn't that gauche. I said it to Brad, but that was bad enough because he made me feel like a first-class idiot. I'd embarrassed him, you see. I was really astonished when he wanted to keep seeing me. Of course, he never took me to a fancy restaurant again.''

"I think you've made too much out of one little incident.''

"Maybe. I was awfully young and naive at the time. But things haven't changed all that much. I'm still not comfortable with the sort of people who have to cleanse their palates between courses.''

"What about your partner?"

"Laurie? What about her?"

"I gather she's quite well-off."

"Laurie's different. She and I were roommates all through college. Money never came into our relationship.''

"It doesn't have to come into any relationship, unless you haven't any money at all."

"If you're trying to play matchmaker, forget it. I'm not interested in Clay Franklin, rich or poor."

"If you say so. It's a pity. There's a tender, loving man underneath all that cynicism. All he needs is to find a caring woman, someone willing to take the time and trouble to coax that side of him back out into the open."

"Why?"

"Why try?"

"Why is he so cynical? Is it just the divorces he handles, or did something happen to him personally?"

"Oh, there was a woman who hurt him once, but I'm sure he's over her by now."

Ariadne found herself pondering her twin's words about Clay as she lay awake later that night, unable to relax enough to go to sleep. *It would hardly have been fair to marry my best friend unless I loved him, too.* Did that mean Clay had been in love with Fay? What if it was Fay herself who had hurt him? Was it her rejection that had made him so cynical?

Groggy from lack of sleep, Ariadne found it all too easy to imagine them together. She'd seen their enthusiastic hug of greeting at the airport and the way he'd held her hand later, in this apartment, because she was upset. When Fay's divorce was final, Clay might well plan to step back into her life. They'd make a striking couple.

Ariadne knew she should be pleased by the prospect of two people she liked finding happiness together. Instead, she was miserable, and more unhappy still when she identified an underlying emotion. In the quiet of the lonely night, even as she told herself that her feelings were the height of foolishness, Ariadne admitted two more terrible truths to herself.

She wanted Clay Franklin.

And she was jealous of her twin.

Chapter Seven

Ariadne was still recovering from the shock of traveling from a mountainous terrain blessed by crisp, below-freezing temperatures, to sea level, where it was hot, humid and energy sapping even this late in the afternoon. She hadn't fully absorbed the fact that her grandparents lived in what appeared to be a crowded but high-class trailer park before Clay pulled into one of a hundred identical driveways and stopped.

The moment she stepped out of the luxurious, air-conditioned rental car, a blast of warm, moist air turned her into a limp noodle. What a great first impression to make on a long-lost family! She was a bedraggled wreck, just when she'd hoped to put her best foot forward, when she was trying to appear calm and collected about meeting her new relatives.

Fay gave her twin a quick smile, squeezed her hand and whispered, "It will be okay. And if I know Nana, she'll have the air conditioner going full blast in there.''

Clay said nothing. He didn't even glance at Ariadne as he got out of the car. Shanna crawled across the front seat to climb out right behind him.

''I don't like this place,'' the little girl announced in a loud and carrying voice. ''It's too hot.''

Ariadne caught and lifted her daughter, whispering to her that they'd be cool again in a minute. The side door, which was shadowed by the roof of a carport, swung open. Shanna abruptly buried her face in her mother's shoulder. Ariadne swallowed hard. There was no going back now. Coming toward her were the people in the photograph, and it had apparently been a recent one, after all.

The couple moved out into the bright Florida sun, but Ariadne's eyes were drawn to George Allandale. She stiffened. Even though he was casually dressed in safari shorts and a short-sleeved cotton shirt that was open at the throat, he possessed a formidable air of command. Calling him the General fit. His gray hair was cut appropriately short and despite the fact that he had to be in his seventies, he didn't have even the hint of a stoop.

As her gaze collided with his, Ariadne glimpsed his first, unguarded reaction—shock. He glanced at her, at Fay and back again as he registered their sameness. Then his expression hardened. The glare he sent her way was full of resentment.

''Hello, Poppa,'' Fay said.

''I thought you weren't coming.'' It sounded like an accusation.

Ariadne blinked in surprise. What on earth was

wrong with the man? He was glowering at Fay and he'd ignored Shanna completely.

"I decided to take a few days off from work." Fay's tone suggested to her sister that she was accustomed to being criticized by her grandfather, that she'd learned to expect this kind of treatment.

"Your husband should be with you if you're taking a vacation," Allandale declared.

Fay shrugged. "What should be and what is aren't always the same thing."

Why didn't Clay speak up in her sister's defense? When Ariadne glanced in his direction she saw that his fists were clenched at his sides, but she did not get the impression that he planned to intervene. As if he felt her gaze upon him, he looked up. His expression conveyed a mixture of emotions—embarrassment, the same irritation she was feeling herself on her sister's behalf…and a resignation that echoed Fay's own attitude.

Rather than address George Allandale, Clay called Ariadne's attention to the woman who had, literally, been standing in George Allandale's shadow. His presence was so overwhelming that she'd simply faded into the background and become invisible. "May I present your grandmother, Ari? This is Lila Allandale."

My grandmother, Ariadne thought.

A gentle smile welcomed her and went a long way toward balancing Ariadne's negative reaction to her newfound grandfather. "Hello, Ariadne," Lila Allandale said. "I'm so glad you've come."

"Thank you." It was difficult to believe that this woman was old enough to have grown granddaughters. Lila looked far too young.

Shanna still had her face hidden. Lila reached out to

touch the little girl's shoulder. "And this must be Shanna."

At the sound of her name, Shanna risked a peek. Lila gasped, one hand flying to her throat.

"Oh, George," she whispered, staring at Ariadne's daughter. "She's the image of Phyllis."

His face showed irritation at being interrupted when he was still browbeating Fay and that did not change when he got his first good look at his great-granddaughter, but his voice was gruff when he spoke again.

"Why are we all standing around outside?" he demanded. "Let's go inside where it's cooler." With one last fulminating glare at Ariadne, he led the way.

A hand touched the small of Ariadne's back. Heat and humidity surrounded her but it was a different kind of warmth that radiated out from that contact point. Clay increased the pressure slightly, to guide her toward the carport. She glanced back at him and their eyes met. A moment of silent communion passed between them. In spite of the fact that he hadn't stood up to Allandale on her sister's behalf, she sensed he was there for her, lending both sympathy and support.

"Is Shanna too heavy for you?" he asked as Fay and Lila obediently trooped after Allandale and left them to bring up the rear. "Do you want me to carry her?"

"I think it's time she got down." Ariadne nuzzled Shanna's cheek with her own. "Pumpkin? Want to walk on your own?"

"I don't like that loud man," Shanna said.

"Good instincts," Clay muttered.

Fighting an urge to turn and run, Ariadne stood Shanna on her own two feet. The little girl slid one hand into her mother's and the other into Clay's and together the three of them went inside.

As promised, the air-conditioning was on full blast. Even better, Lila had waited for them in the kitchen, which was just inside the door. It was full of good smells.

"I've made a light supper," she told Ariadne. "I know I'm always starving when I get home from a trip."

Shanna was clinging to her mother's legs again. "Mommy," she whined. "I've got to pee."

Lila chuckled. "And that's usually the other priority."

As soon as Ariadne and Shanna rejoined the others, Ariadne looked for Clay. He stood at the open sliding door to the Florida room, staring out at the street. She got the disquieting impression that he was trying to distance himself from whatever was about to happen. She wondered if she'd been hasty in thinking she could depend on him.

Squaring her shoulders, prepared to look out for herself, she searched next for George Allandale. He sat enthroned on an overstuffed recliner, clearly the most comfortable piece of furniture in the living room. Lila perched at the edge of her seat on a small, upright chair to his right. With skillful fingers she was plying an embroidery needle on a piece of linen held tight in a round hoop. Fay had claimed the sofa, leaving room for her sister and niece. She patted the cushions beside her as soon as she caught sight of them.

Quelling her reluctance to spend any time at all in Allandale's formidable presence, Ariadne sat down. She started to lift Shanna onto her lap, but her daughter had other plans.

"Look, Mommy. A cat." A ragged collection of bones and fur came staggering past Clay and into the living room. Shanna attempted to intercept the wretched-looking beast.

"Don't touch him," Allandale commanded.

Undisturbed by the loud, sharp voice, the cat wove his unsteady way to Allandale's chair. With surprisingly gentle hands, the old man scooped him up and settled him on his knees. A buzz-saw purr filled the awkward silence in the room.

"That's Rover," Fay said. "Nana's cat."

Nana's cat? There was a polite fiction if ever Ariadne had heard one. Owning a cat probably didn't suit George Allandale's image of himself.

Shanna stared at man and animal a moment longer, then gravitated toward her great-grandmother. Abandoning her needlework, Lila opened her arms. To Ariadne's surprise, Shanna went into them without hesitation.

As she tucked the little girl in next to her on the chair, Lila blinked suspiciously moist eyes. "You'll have to forgive your great-granddaddy," she told Shanna. "That poor old cat is nearly twenty years old and fragile and George does tend to be protective. He's very good with animals. We used to have a dog, years ago. George nursed old Skippy through two strokes."

"She doesn't need to hear about Skippy, Lila."

"I'm sorry, George."

Good with animals and lousy with people, Ariadne thought. She had to remind herself again that she was supposed to be keeping an open mind about her new family.

"Are you too warm, Ariadne?" Lila asked. "Fay

always complains about how humid it is here in Florida, so we turned the air on before you arrived."

"I'm fine, thank you."

"Maine. We were in Maine once. Weren't we, George?"

His bright blue eyes, the only light-colored pair in the family, were cold as the temperatures back home. "We didn't care for the place," he said. And then, for the first time, he spoke directly to Ariadne. "Would you live that far north if you had any choice?"

"I have no complaints about my home," she told him.

"But then you've never had the chance to live anywhere else. You would if you could."

Biting back a sharp retort, Ariadne kept a tight rein on her temper. Taking everyone's agreement for granted seemed to be something George Allandale did as a matter of course. Even when he asked a question, he answered it himself, apparently convinced that no one could possibly disagree. Ariadne told herself she was too polite to argue with him. In truth, she was too wary of his skill with the barbed comment. It was a relief when Lila announced that supper was ready.

A shuffleboard trophy caught Ariadne's eye as she passed it on the way to the table. Curious to see which grandparent was the champion, she stopped to take a closer look, but neither name was inscribed on the base. The trophy had been won by a stranger.

Still puzzling over this odd discovery, she was startled when Clay came up behind her to pull out her chair. A half turn had them nearly touching. His lips were only an inch from her ear.

"They bought the place furnished," he whispered. "Pots and pans, knickknacks and all."

His fingers brushed her shoulders as she took her seat, driving every thought of mysterious trophies right out of her mind. She was acutely aware that he was sitting next to her throughout the meal. His presence added the steady hum of sexual tension to an already highly charged atmosphere.

Ariadne had never thought of herself as claustrophobic, but she couldn't seem to shake off a sense of being hemmed in. Although she tried to convince herself that she was just overtired and nervous, she could feel the antagonism flowing toward her from George Allandale's end of the table in an almost tangible wave.

Imagination? She wanted to believe that, but the resistance she encountered simply trying to carry on a polite conversation convinced her there was real antipathy at work here. Every time she asked a perfectly normal question and Lila started to give more than the briefest of answers, Allandale rudely cut her off.

Soon Ariadne was frustrated and fuming. Allandale interrupted Lila in a condescending way, which left the impression that her opinions were worthless. To Ariadne's amazement, Lila didn't appear to take offense and once or twice she even apologized to him. Fay behaved in much the same conciliatory way, and if she minded her grandfather's constant put-downs, she didn't let it show.

Ariadne minded on their behalf, almost as much as she resented Allandale's none-too-subtle attempts to interrogate her about Shanna's father. He pelted questions at her until she felt like an inexperienced kid on a first-job interview. She was being weighed and evaluated…and found wanting.

If Shanna hadn't begun to chatter away to Lila, telling her about day care and her friend Mary Sue, Ariadne suspected she'd have lost her temper long before they finished their simple meal. Clay must have sensed how close she was to exploding. He glanced pointedly at his watch the moment they finished dessert and announced that they needed to go check in at the hotel.

"Fay will be staying here with us," Allandale said.

For the first time since their arrival, Ariadne's sister objected to what her grandfather said. "I don't want to crowd you. Besides, I'd planned to—"

"Change your plans." With a jerk of his head, Allandale indicated that he wanted to talk to Fay alone, but there was no real privacy in a place so small. Ariadne heard the words *divorce* and *Gary* quite clearly and wasn't at all surprised when Fay reappeared, announced she was staying, and retrieved her suitcases from the car.

After hasty good-nights, Ariadne, Shanna and Clay left her there. A giddy feeling of freedom overcame Ariadne the moment she stepped outside, erasing any vestige of guilt she might have felt at abandoning Fay. They'd come back for her. In the meantime, she felt as if she'd just escaped from jail. No, she quickly corrected herself. She'd been released, but she was still on probation.

"It's a suite." The look Clay saw in Ari's eyes made her words into an accusation.

"Yes," he said calmly. "It is a suite. Do you have a problem with that?"

They were talking in whispers. Shanna had fallen asleep in the car and they didn't want to wake her. Clay took the little girl from her mother's arms and carried her into the largest bedroom, placing her gently on one of the two double beds. Ari brought the suitcase with

Shanna's clothes and a canvas bag that contained toys, games and coloring books.

"Why don't you get her settled for the night. Then come have a nightcap with me. Juice," he added, remembering that she didn't drink.

"There you go, taking over again," Ari grumbled.

"Ari, it's my job." And he'd wanted her to have the best. And he'd wanted to stay close to her. A suite had seemed the ideal solution.

"I don't like bossy men."

"Me?" He grinned at her, hoping to tease her into better humor.

"When you said you'd handle booking the hotel room, I never expected all this."

No. She'd have been happy with a budget motel. Before she could start a lecture on the virtues of frugality or, worse, offer to pay her share of the expense, Clay placed one finger across her lips to silence her. "It's not costing anything, Ari. This suite belongs to a friend of mine. Or rather, to his company."

"A corporate suite?" She sounded doubtful and looked flustered. He hoped the latter was a reaction to his touch.

"We have these rooms for the entire week, free of charge." What he did not tell her was that the suite had been provided by George Allandale, who just happened to own this hotel.

Leaving her to get Shanna settled, Clay poured himself a stiff drink from the well-stocked bar, then sat on the sofa, waiting for Ari to emerge from the room she'd be sharing with her daughter. Unfortunately, that gave him time to think.

He didn't like anything about George Allandale's scheme. The old man insisted he was trying to protect

Fay, and her inheritance, but his claim that Ari was "just like her father" was ludicrous. George had gone to extreme lengths to keep Ari from glimpsing the luxury of his real home, which would have betrayed the fact that the family had money. In order to keep his granddaughter in the dark while he "tested" her, he and Lila had moved into a middle-class retirement community and were pretending they lived there year-round.

Clay downed the rest of his drink and was thinking about pouring another when he heard Ari say, "I'll leave the door open." Clay had just time enough to compose his features before she swept into the living room of the suite like a breath of fresh air.

"She woke up, but I'm hoping she'll drift right off again," Ari announced as she gave their luxurious surroundings another once-over as she picked up the glass of orange juice he'd left for her on the bar. She seemed to have lost any desire to argue with him and sank wearily into the love seat opposite his sofa without further comment.

Even as worn-out as she must be after traveling most of two days, meeting family she'd never known existed and coping with George's open hostility, she looked wonderful to him.

The drink, he abruptly realized, had been a bad idea. It had weakened his willpower and sharpened his libido. He wanted to go over there and sit next to Ari and, as he had that night in her apartment, take her in his arms and offer comfort. And more. It was going to be an effort to keep his hands to himself.

"You dealt very well with your grandfather," he said. Talking about George ought to kill any romantic notions.

"I didn't like him much, to be perfectly honest. I wanted to, Clay. I really did. But he's so manipulative. And almost every comment he made to his wife or to my sister was the kind that undermines a person's self-confidence. Why is he like that, Clay?"

"Damned if I know." He admired the way she'd caught on to George's tricks so fast, so much so that not even talking about that conniving old man could keep his mind off the sexual pull he felt toward her. Stupid. Making love to Ari would undoubtedly be pleasurable, but not at all smart.

"Someone should stand up to him," she said. "That's the only way to deal with a bully."

"Sometimes that just makes the bully madder." She frowned, making him wonder if he'd disappointed her. "I'm no knight in shining armor, Ari. I don't fight dragons to rescue fair maidens."

"Not even Fay?"

"Once in a while I try to run interference between George and Fay," he told her, "but that's about it. Besides, Fay prefers that I mind my own business. Take my advice, Ari. Let your sister deal with your grandfather in her own way."

There were times when Fay did so quite effectively, he thought. She'd waged a royal battle with George on the subject of contacting Ari. If she was content most of the time to smooth things over and let George run the show, Clay couldn't think any less of her for that.

A grim smile settled over his features as he suddenly remembered something his mother had said a few years ago. It had been shortly after Clay's father filed for divorce. Lila had come by, full of sympathy. When she'd left, Clay's mother had remarked that there went one of those rare women who'd be lucky if her husband *did* divorce her. Clay had thought at the time that his mother was exaggerating. He'd changed his mind tonight.

"I don't have Fay's patience," Ari lamented as she sipped her juice. "If it weren't for the fact that Shanna seems to like Lila so much, I'd pack and go home tonight."

Rotating her shoulders, then her head, Ari tried to work out some of the kinks she'd acquired during the long, tiring day. Renewed desire shot through Clay, propelling him across the space between sofa and love seat before he had time to think better of the impulse.

"Move over and turn around." Hands on her shoulders, he positioned her the way he wanted her. "Fortunately for you, Ms. Palmer, I'm a world champion in the category of Olympic neck rub."

Her first startled protest turned into a moan of pleasure as he began to massage her tight muscles. With a hand that shook slightly, she set her half-empty orange juice glass down on the coffee table.

Accepting that he was unable to keep his hands off her entirely, Clay now fought to restrict their forays to her neck and shoulders. What he really wanted was to let his fingers drift forward over her breasts. Then he'd turn her in his arms and touch her everywhere.

Every breathy, contented little sound she made reminded him of how much he liked to hear her speak in that sexy, husky voice of hers. If she'd asked him to make love to her right then, he'd have been unable to resist.

But Ari said nothing, only continued to make those arousing sighs and moans as he brought her relief from the aches and pains in her neck. She felt wonderful

n his hands. Soft but firm. Wonderfully respon-
Her delicate perfume was driving him wild.

This has to stop.

He didn't want to release her, but in another moment
she would certainly become aware of just how powerfully she'd affected him. If she responded positively
to discovering the obvious proof that he desired her, he
wasn't sure he'd be able to remember all the reasons
why getting more involved with her was such a bad
idea.

"Clay?"

He blinked. That wasn't passion in her voice, but
pain. He'd been using too much force on her shoulders.

"Better?" He kneaded for a moment longer. When
he finally forced himself to lift his hands away from
her, to stop touching her entirely, he was surprised she
hadn't objected sooner. He'd been applying so much
pressure that his thumbs had gone numb.

"That was heavenly. Thank you." She turned to
face him, her eyes meeting his just as their knees
brushed.

Everything she felt was reflected in the depths of
those dark, luminous pools. Her pupils widened, revealing equal parts of surprise and confusion and
arousal.

"I should go check on Shanna," she whispered, but
she made no effort to get up and leave.

The air around them crackled, charged with the force
of the electricity between them. His gaze still locked
on hers, Clay kept his movements slow, giving her
plenty of time to run away, but as he leaned in toward
her, she swayed in his direction.

Their lips met with an explosion of mutual need. He
didn't think he'd ever tasted anything so delicious. A

trace of orange juice lingered on her lips, and beneath it was the taste that was pure Ariadne. It went to his head faster than twelve-year-old Scotch.

Intent on deepening the kiss, he was so shocked when she pushed at his chest and pulled away that he let her slip out of his embrace without a struggle. Once again, confusion warred with desire in the depths of her dark eyes. Bemused, she lifted her fingertips to her lips. "This isn't a good idea," she said.

That husky voice was nearly enough to make him discount what she was saying and respond only to the longing he heard beneath the words, but Clay was still rational enough to know he agreed with her, even if he was having trouble recalling why. He'd never wanted a woman as badly as he wanted this one.

Not even Barbara.

Memories surfaced with a vengeance, forcefully reminding him just why he had to guard against being taken in by a pretty face and a trim figure. The past crashed over him like the sea at high tide, dashing any vestige of optimism against the rocks.

Women had an infinite capacity for deceit. They might not all be motivated by the same things, but they were always after something. And never satisfied. Cynicism had one advantage. You couldn't be disappointed if you looked for the worst in the first place.

For a few minutes he'd forgotten the lessons Barbara had taught him, forgotten that she'd played him for a fool. Clay forced himself to remember everything, and think about what Barbara was doing to his father now.

There was trouble in paradise, even though Clayton senior hadn't been willing to admit it. Barbara was making him miserable. "We'll work it out," he'd assured his son just yesterday. That meant he intended to give in to whatever demands Barbara was making.

Clay felt his lip curl in contempt. That was what all marriages seemed to come down to. Compromise, they called it. Better to divorce. Or avoid marrying in the first place. The only relationships that seemed to last were those in which one partner was willing to be the other's doormat.

He'd been staring at Ari without seeing her. Now he shifted his focus to her face and found Barbara's features superimposed upon it. That there was little physical resemblance between them didn't mean there weren't similarities.

Blinded by her apparent openness and honesty, he'd come to admire Ari's independent streak without ever making the connection. It had been Barbara's self-reliance that had first attracted him to her, too. In Barbara's case, the quality had masked an innate selfishness.

What was Ariadne Palmer's hidden agenda?

The possibility that she had none crossed his mind but he shunted it aside.

It was much safer for his peace of mind to continue to believe the worst of her.

"You're right. This isn't a good idea." He wondered why he wanted so badly to have her contradict him.

"I wish I knew what you were thinking," she said, surprising him. "You seem almost angry that you kissed me."

Angry at himself, he silently agreed, for losing control. There was one way to make sure it never happened again.

"Making love to me won't lead anywhere," he

warned, "except to a brief, casual affair. Somehow I don't think that's what you want."

She left his side in a rush, but not before he'd recognized the anguish in her eyes.

For a long time after she'd fled, Clay stared at the closed door to the room she shared with her daughter, trying to convince himself that he'd been right to be blunt and honest with her. He'd told her the truth. Ever since Barbara's betrayal, he hadn't wanted anything to do with complex romantic relationships.

And he didn't want anything more to do with complex deceptions, either. Tomorrow, he vowed, he'd confront George Allandale and convince the old man to release him from his promise.

Once Ari knew the truth, she'd show her true colors quickly enough. If there was a mercenary soul concealed inside that beautiful body, she wouldn't be able to hide it much longer. If she was really what she seemed, that would come out, too. Either way, there would be no more secrets. No more lies.

He could go back to his old life. He could forget the way Ari had felt in his arms. In time, if it turned out that she was what she seemed, he would start to think of her as he thought of Fay—as an honorary sister. He could be Shanna's uncle instead of her extra daddy.

The picture he'd been painting in his mind abruptly shattered. Visualizing the future the way he visualized presenting a client's case in court wasn't working. That realization brought with it a disturbing insight. He was convincing as a divorce lawyer because he could always persuade himself that his client was the injured party, that they had right on their side. He prided himself on his ability to win by presenting the truth.

How long ago, he wondered now, had he learned the art of lying to himself?

Chapter Eight

Fay phoned the hotel suite at eight the next morning to announce that Lila had planned an outing. "She's packed a huge picnic lunch," Ariadne's twin said. "Please say you'll come. I know you're thinking you'll roast outside on a day like this, but it isn't really that hot. It just seems that way since we're used to winter. And I promise that there will be a nice cooling breeze coming in off the gulf."

"I can endure a little heat and humidity," Ariadne assured her. She considered that a small price to pay in order to avoid another bout of the claustrophobia she'd experienced trying to "visit" indoors. Maybe this family reunion business would go more smoothly if there was room to breathe.

A frown darkened her features when she'd hung up. It was difficult to feel optimistic this morning when she'd slept so poorly the night before. Dreams had troubled her again—nightmares featuring George Allandale and erotic fantasies born out of that last frustrating encounter with Clay. He was quiet this morning, she noticed, saying little. She left him alone with his coffee and his newspaper.

At midmorning they all met at a public park. At first, Ariadne's grandfather seemed more amiable than before, especially when he noticed that she'd brought her 35mm camera along. "Phyllis was a professional photographer at your age." He named a national magazine, then spoiled the moment by adding, "She didn't work there long. Didn't work at anything long. Photography was just another little hobby, and she got bored after a while."

Ariadne wasn't sure how to react. Why had he told her something positive about her mother only to turn right around and run her down? That he sent a bitter, accusing look in her direction was even more confusing. Surely he couldn't blame her for his daughter's failure to find a steady job.

At least he was talking to her. She reminded herself again that she was staying for Shanna's sake. Shanna and Lila had made a connection and Ariadne did not want to break it. She could put up with Allandale in order to maintain that other, more important relationship. It was only for a few days. But she had to close her eyes and count to ten when he began to instruct her on the best way to frame a photograph of Shanna helping Lila set the table for their picnic. Forcing a smile, she snapped two shots exactly as he wanted them, then took a third picture to suit herself.

"Now take that photo."

Something in Allandale's voice warned her that she might not like what she was going to see. Following his line of vision, her gaze collided with her sister and Clay. They stood close together beneath a cypress tree as they talked. She had one hand on his forearm. The pose spoke of casual intimacy born of long friendship.

Or of love.

Was that why he'd warned her off last night? Was he in love with Fay? Ariadne had known all along that Clay's feelings for her sister ran deep. Was it so far-fetched to believe that he'd once wanted to marry her?

Maybe he still did.

"Make a nice-looking couple, don't they?"

Ariadne waited for her grandfather to add something negative.

"I've always thought Clay was the right man for her."

"What happened to wanting her to reconcile with Gary?"

"Fay deserves the best." His cold blue eyes narrowed, pinning her, making her feel like an inferior specimen in a butterfly collection. "I've seen the way you look at that boy. He's not for you, Ariadne. In fact, there's nothing here for you."

"I don't recall asking for anything. In fact, I'm only here because you invited me."

When he looked thoughtful rather than contemptuous, Ariadne experienced a moment's hope that he might be mellowing. At the least he might explain his antipathy toward her. But he closed himself off again, his eyes bleak. Gesturing toward the couple beneath the tree, he ordered her to take their picture.

"Since you asked so nicely," she retorted. Turning her back on him, she framed the shot.

Clay had braced one hand against the tree, leaning in toward her sister, who was now toying with something in her hands. That the two of them made a picture-perfect couple was peculiarly painful. His blond, all-American-boy good looks contrasted sharply with Fay's dark beauty. If Ariadne pretended she was looking into a mirror instead of through a viewfinder, she could almost believe she was seeing herself there with Clay.

She looks just like me. It still came as a shock to be faced with this other person who was her double.

Had Clay ever told Phaedra that the most he would share with her was a brief, casual affair? Ariadne didn't think so. In fact, the more she considered their situation, the more reasonable it seemed to her that he'd jump at the chance to offer Fay marriage. Just following legendary precedent, she thought glumly. After all, in the myth, Theseus seduced Ariadne but married her sister, Phaedra.

Be happy for them, she ordered herself as she snapped the picture. She decided that such a feat would be much easier to accomplish if she didn't keep a print of this particular photograph.

"So, the marriage counselor hasn't been much help," Fay concluded as she twisted and untwisted a malleable cotton sun visor into a variety of tortured shapes. The brim would never be the same again. "I don't know whether to go ahead with the divorce or not." She looked up at Clay and managed a wry smile. "Of course, Poppa has no doubts about what I should do. He gave me quite a lecture last night after you three left."

"I'll bet." Ari had hit the nail on the head. The old man did tend to browbeat Fay. And Lila. And anyone else who would let him.

"I reminded him that he wasn't always so enthusiastic. Remember? He tried his darnedest to find something wrong with Gary before we got married."

"Do you know what George told me at your wedding?" Clay asked. "He said that since I wouldn't settle down and take care of his little girl's little girl, Gary would have to do. I think he was trying to make me jealous. He pointed out that the Vandemanns were almost as old and respectable as the Franklins, even if Gary did have to trace his roots back to the first Dutch settlers in New York rather than to the *Mayflower*."

"He'd 'do'?" Fay chuckled. "Apparently he's gone up in Poppa's estimation since then. Either that or he just can't stand the idea of another divorce in the family."

Gary hadn't "done" at all in Clay's opinion. Vandemann was completely self-involved, more dedicated to his various scholarly research projects than to his wife. He didn't want a family. Children would distract him, he said. He'd probably been smart enough never to say that in front of George Allandale, though. Otherwise George wouldn't still think he was such a "suitable" husband for his granddaughter. In the past, George had also used the term "good breeding stock" in connection with Fay's husband. Clay wondered why, if George had his eye on posterity, he hadn't taken more interest in Shanna.

"I thought I knew what I was doing when I left Gary," Fay murmured as she reached up to adjust the collar of Clay's shirt. "But I didn't expect to feel so lonely."

"That's not a very good reason to stay shackled to him. Get a cat." Fay smacked him on the arm. It was no gentle, playful tap but a full-force wallop. "What? You've got something against cats?"

"That's not the point." She sighed deeply. "I'll figure out what I want to do soon. I just need time. If everything hadn't happened at once...the breakup with Gary, Mother dying, finding out I had a twin...I'd probably have my life all in perfect working order by now. At least the job's going well," she added brightly.

Clay didn't respond. He'd made the mistake of glancing toward the picnic area where the others were gathered. His gaze found Ari, locked on her and would not be dislodged. She appeared to be taking happy family pictures of George and Lila and Shanna, but he scarcely noticed what they were doing. Every fiber of his being responded to the sight of Ariadne, caught in a brilliant ray of sunlight.

Each sensuous curve of her shapely silhouette seemed to be outlined in gold. She hadn't worn anything overtly sexy for their outing in the park, just a pair of cotton slacks and a fancy T-shirt, but they hugged her form enticingly. Her raven's wing hair gleamed, swinging freely as she shifted for a better angle. Clay's body hardened in a rush.

"So, what's with you and my sister?"

"I wish I knew. It's confusing looking at her, seeing your face and body, and feeling..." Clay let his voice trail off, unable to find the proper words to describe all that Ari did to him.

"Lust?" Fay suggested.

"Oh, yeah. Definitely lust."

"I think it's more than that."

"Isn't that bad enough? A relationship between your sister and me is not a good idea."

"Why not?"

He'd asked himself the same question all night long, so he had all the reasons ready. "There are still unanswered questions about her."

Dismissing that objection with a wave of her hand, Fay leaned close again. "If you're attracted to each other, I think you should see where it leads. I'm convinced she's exactly what she appears to be. Give her the benefit of the doubt."

This from the woman who'd once thought Gary Vandemann was a prize. "She has a child," he reminded her.

"Not a problem. Shanna adores you. And you'll always be Aunt Fay's friend no matter what happens between you and Ari. Any other arguments?"

"Stop matchmaking, Fay. You've forgotten that Ari still hasn't been told the truth about the situation here. If she is as honest as she appears, she's going to be devastated at the deception when it comes out."

Abruptly sobering, Fay frowned. "There is that. Tell her, Clay. She'll find out eventually and it will be better if she hears it from you."

"Better for whom?"

"Everyone. You're already involved, whether you want to admit it or not. Tell her before things get any more complicated." She grinned up at him, mischief in her eyes. "Tell her, and then enjoy yourselves. You both deserve to have someone special in your lives."

Bound by his word, Clay had allowed George to manipulate him as well as Ari. He'd already planned to ask to be released from what amounted to a vow of secrecy. Talking to Fay reinforced his need to be freed from it.

After lunch, he decided, as they heard Lila's cheerful shout. "Come and get it," she called.

Clay turned away from Phaedra and walked toward Ariadne.

When the picnic lunch had been devoured and the remains cleared away, George Allandale suggested the "womenfolk" might enjoy a walk through the park's botanical gardens while he and Clay stayed behind and enjoyed a cigar.

"Poppa's variation of a fine old British tradition," Fay said with a chuckle. "Ladies in the parlor so the gentlemen can retire after dinner for their smelly cigars and a glass or two of brandy."

Ariadne barely heard her. "I forgot the sunscreen," she murmured. Both she and Shanna needed a fresh application. Even here in the tree-shaded park, the Florida sunshine was more than they were accustomed to. "You go on," she urged. "I know right where I left it."

She didn't see anyone else around when she grabbed up the brightly colored tube she'd left on the picnic table, but as she turned away she heard the rumble of male voices. The two men had walked down over the small rise, to a point from which they could look out over the shore. Ariadne meant to leave without speaking to them, but she hesitated when she heard her own name.

"Does Ariadne get enough out of Shanna's father to take proper care of that child?" George asked.

Ariadne wanted to tell him it was none of his business, but before she could make her presence known, Clay answered for her. "Ari has an adequate income from her business and Shanna's child-support money is in the bank for her college expenses."

How, Ariadne wondered, had he known that?

"I'd have thought she'd have insisted on a big set-tlement," Allandale mused. "Duncan Lourdes says the fellow looks like he can afford it."

Well, that answered her question. She still felt her blood begin to boil every time she remembered that a private detective had grilled Shanna.

"I don't think this is something you want to get into with Ariadne," Clay continued. "I can tell you right now that she thinks putting a monetary value on everything is a terrible way to live."

"Haven't you ever heard that a woman can't be too thin or too rich?"

"I've heard that. I just don't believe it." After a brief pause he added in a thoughtful voice, "I doubt Ari has ever been on a diet in her life."

In spite of her irritation at Allandale, Ariadne found herself smiling. It seemed that Clay had a bit of the knight in shining armor in him, after all. She knew she should move on, but the fact that the two of them were talking about her behind her back seemed to justify her own breach of good manners. Besides, there was too much that was puzzling her about her grandfather. She might learn something if she stayed put. She told herself that her lurking presence behind a huge, flowering azalea bush had nothing to do with her desire to hear more of Clay's opinions of her.

"Give her the benefit of the doubt, why don't you, George?"

"Why should I? I made an effort with her father, and look how that turned out."

"Did you? All I've ever heard you say about Mark Palmer was that he was a mercenary bastard who ruined your little girl."

"Well, he was," Allandale insisted. "A good-for-nothing bum!'' Ariadne barely stopped herself from crying out in protest. ''What do you know about it, anyway? For that matter, how much can Ariadne know? Mark Palmer died when she was three.''

''She may not have known her father, but she was brought up by his father. According to Ari, a more honest man never lived.''

Allandale snorted derisively. ''That honest man who lied to her?''

''There's the pot calling the kettle black,'' Clay told him.

Trembling, Ariadne began to move away, suddenly desperate to escape before she betrayed her presence. Struggling to get a grip on her temper, she told herself that her two grandfathers couldn't be expected to say anything good about each other. With an effort, Ariadne calmed down enough to acknowledge that Gramps had been just as unfair as Allandale was. He'd blamed her mother for everything. Allandale blamed her father.

As silently as she'd come upon them, she carefully crept away, shaken to the core by her realization that she'd come to Florida, at least in part, with the naive notion that a new grandfather might somehow help make up for losing Gramps. That had been the real reason she'd wanted to like George Allandale. And it was the real reason she was so upset by overhearing this conversation and discovering the depth of his dislike for her.

Ten minutes later, Clay was losing the battle to keep a civil tongue as he tried to talk sense into George Allandale. The man refused to listen to reason and he would not release Clay from his promise. He insisted he was not yet through "testing" Ari.

At first he thought he was imagining the tug on his shirttail, but the second time was hard enough to convince him it was real. He looked down. Troubled but expectant brown eyes gazed back at him.

"What's wrong, Shanna?"

"Mommy's crying," the four-year-old said.

Clay's heart melted. He didn't know what he'd done to win this little girl's trust, but it was there in her eyes, an infinitely precious gift. She smiled at him, confident that he could fix whatever it was that was troubling Ari. He could only hope her faith was justified.

"Where's your mommy?"

Shanna pointed. Across an expanse of grassy park he caught sight of a flutter of bright-colored material beneath the same cypress tree where he'd stood earlier, talking to Fay. Ari was sitting on the ground, half-concealed by the tree trunk. She looked as if she might not want company, but he didn't want to let Shanna down.

"Okay, pumpkin. I'll go talk to her." With his heel, he ground out the stub of the cigar he hadn't really wanted, then pocketed the remains to be disposed of later.

"Make her stop being sad."

"I'll try," he promised. "Do you know where your aunt Fay is?" Shanna nodded. "Go and stay with her, okay?"

With another nod, Shanna started to race off in the opposite direction.

"Wait just a minute!" George's command was issued through a cloud of cigar smoke.

Shanna came to a screeching halt and looked back,

half scared, half fascinated. Clay winked at her. George's ire was directed at him, not the child.

"You don't just let a kid that age go haring off unsupervised." A bit stiffly, George held one hand out to Shanna. "I'll take you to your great-grandmother and your aunt," he said in a low, gruff voice that betrayed more than he realized. The old man, Clay thought with surprise, had a soft spot, after all.

Warily, Shanna approached her great-grandfather. She glanced at Clay again, waiting for his nod before she'd accept the proffered hand. With mixed feelings he watched them walk away together. It wasn't that he didn't trust George to take good care of her. It was that he wanted to be the one who was responsible for Shanna's well-being.

The thought shook him.

It also reminded him that he'd promised Shanna he'd check on her mommy.

Shanna had been right. Ari was crying. She sat on the ground beneath the tree, silent tears streaming down her cheeks, staring off into the distance. She did not look his way even though he deliberately made a good deal of noise on his approach.

"Fay always tells me I'm a good listener," he said when he was hunkered down beside her. "If you want to talk, I'm here for you."

She accepted the handkerchief he offered but didn't seem to know what to do with it. Clay took it back and gently dried her cheeks. Then he pushed it into her hand. "Blow your nose," he told her.

Ari managed a weak smile after she'd followed his orders. "You always seem to show up when I'm at my worst."

"Shanna was worried about you." He braced one

hand on the grassy ground and felt the individual blades make their impression on his palm. "Want to tell me what's wrong?"

"I'm just being foolish."

"You're not a foolish woman, Ari." He shifted position so that he could wrap an arm around her shoulders and pull her back to lean against the tree trunk. The rough bark bit into his back, but he ignored the discomfort. It was nothing compared to the sweet torture of having her pressed against his side.

Holding her close was probably a mistake, but she needed him. Needed to be cuddled a little. He'd just have to suffer. "Why were you crying?"

"It's just…everything."

"Can you be a little more specific?"

She started to nestle against him, then realized what she was doing and went perfectly still, holding herself stiffly even though she didn't actually move away. The small rejection was exquisitely painful but he supposed he deserved to be hurt. He'd wounded her last night with his crass words and inexplicable coldness. Of course she was wary of him now.

"If you're crying over my behavior," he said with a trace of bitterness, "I'm not worth it."

He felt each reaction. She was startled, then, almost in spite of herself, amused. "What conceit. I was feeling sorry for myself, if you must know. I built up too many expectations about my newly discovered grandfather. I guess I was hoping he'd be more like Gramps. Turns out he doesn't even like me."

"I won't make excuses for him. I couldn't if I wanted to. Would it help to think about him as the rain that must fall into each life?"

That won him a chuckle that was eerily similar to

Fay's. "Good advice. Have you always been this smart about people?"

"No," he admitted. "At least once, I was very, very wrong."

Keep it light, he warned himself. *And don't even think about kissing her again.*

Their eyes met, held, faltered. "Time to go reassure Shanna that you've stopped being sad," he said.

She looked as if she wanted to object but in the end she said nothing, just accepted his hand to help her rise and walked with him back to the others.

By the time they piled into the cars to drive back to the Allandales', Ariadne felt wary as a skater on thin ice. It wasn't just her grandfather who set her teeth on edge. Clay contributed to the tension, too. She was finding it hard to reconcile what he'd once said about himself—*No kids. No wife. Never have had. Never will.*—with what she saw when she watched him with Shanna. Or with what she'd felt when he'd offered her, literally, a shoulder to cry on.

She glanced over at him as he drove. Hair mussed by the breeze made him look as if he'd just rolled out of bed.

Stop it, she warned herself. He'd been honest with her. The best she could hope for between them was a brief, casual affair. Unfortunately, even that was beginning to sound tempting. She'd never been this strongly attracted to any other man. Part of her wanted to explore the possibilities.

Clay turned off the highway and slowed to a decorous fifteen-mile-an-hour speed limit ensured by gigantic speed bumps. "What does that sign say?" Shanna asked, pointing as they passed through the entrance to the retirement community where the Allandales lived.

"Hilltop Heights," Ariadne told her.

"Where's the hill?"

"Good question. Looks flat to me."

"Apparently there's an elevation here that's a few feet above sea level," Clay said. She could hear the smile in his voice. "In these parts, that counts as a hill."

They passed a swimming pool enclosed by a stone wall, a squat, square stucco building that served as a clubhouse, and a shuffleboard court before taking the third left to enter a side street. "Mommy, Aunt Fay said she'd take me swimming in the pool. Can I go?"

"You don't have a suit," Ariadne reminded her. She didn't add that she intended to find an excuse to go back to their hotel just as soon as possible. She'd about reached her limit for one day. A little distance from George Allandale and she might be able to start fresh again tomorrow. For Shanna's sake, and Lila's, she hoped so.

Seeing her grandmother and her daughter together was pure pleasure. Ariadne had never had a grandmother to spoil her when she was a child, though Miss Emily had occasionally filled in. She wanted Shanna to experience everything she had missed.

That was the only reason why, when it turned out that Lila had gone out and bought a swimsuit for Shanna, Ariadne found she couldn't object to Fay taking the little girl for a swim. She looked adorable in a bright red one-piece with a frilly skirt.

"What do you say to your great-grandmother?" Allandale prompted.

"Thank you, Great-Grandmother," Shanna said.

"Call her Nana, the way Fay does," Allandale ordered.

"Thank you, Nana."

"And what do you call your great-grandfather?"

"Bumpa," Shanna answered promptly, a big smile on her face.

A premonition sent Ariadne forward, but it was already too late.

"Then you'll call me Bumpa from now on," Allandale said.

Shanna burst into tears.

"What? What's wrong with you, girl?"

"You're not Bumpa!" Shanna wailed.

"Of course he isn't." Ariadne gathered her sobbing daughter close and murmured soothing comfort words. She almost felt sorry for George Allandale...until he opened his mouth.

"Doesn't the child know her other grandfather is dead?" he demanded. "Stop making all that fuss, young lady. Stop it, I say."

"Don't you dare try to boss her around!" Ferocious in defense of her young, Ariadne glared at him until he retreated, grumbling about rudeness and lack of respect.

Although she was peripherally aware that Allandale had scooped Rover up and was holding the cat, stroking his fur as he stood at the sliding glass doors and glowered at the world at large, Ariadne ignored him. She concentrated on getting Shanna calmed down.

"Do you still want to go for a swim?" she asked when the sniffling finally stopped.

Shanna nodded.

"Into a cover-up, then." Fay appeared beside them

with a red-and-white terry-cloth robe. Her own swim-suit was modestly covered by one of pale blue.

The room had gotten very quiet now that Shanna was no longer carrying on. Ariadne glanced around, wondering if everyone had left. George was still by the door. Lila sat in a corner, out of the line of fire, her fingers busy with a piece of fancy needlework. Clay lounged in the archway that led to the kitchen, watching everything and saying nothing. Unable to read his expression, Ariadne hastily looked away.

Clay had taken no part in the Bumpa battle, except to stay close in case Ari needed him. A wry smile surfaced at this evidence of his own conceit. She didn't need anyone. His admiration for her increased when he watched her see Shanna and Fay off to the pool, then approach her grandfather to hold out an olive branch.

"I'm sorry if I was rude earlier. I meant no disrespect."

Metaphorically, he took that olive branch and smacked her upside the head with it. "Sorry doesn't help."

Aware of the effort it must be taking for Ari to hang on to her temper, Clay quickly moved to her side, but once again she proved she didn't need his help. Her voice was chillingly calm as she took one last stab at making peace.

"If you want Shanna to accept that you're her great-grandfather," she said, "you'll have to be patient with her. And find another name for her to call you. She knows all too well that Bumpa isn't coming back."

A contemptuous snort was George's answer. "If she'd had a proper upbringing, she'd know how to behave."

"She wasn't exactly raised in a barn," Ari retorted,

"and neither was I. You can stop acting as if you've stepped in something that smells bad every time you have to speak to me."

Clay winced. Ari wasn't about to let anyone get away with criticizing her child. Unfortunately, she and George both possessed the type of tempers that fed off each other.

"You're insolent," George accused. "Just like your father."

For a moment, Ari was at a loss for words, mouth slack, eyes wide. Then her jaw snapped shut and she gave as good as she got. "If he was insolent to you, I'm sure he had good reason to be. What did he do? Stand up for his wife?"

"He threatened to take Phyllis away from me."

"Too bad she wouldn't go."

An awful silence fell. Eyes locked, George and Ari stared at each other like prizefighters facing off.

Clay held his breath. George was not going to back down. Being right or wrong had nothing to do with it.

Ari was the first to blink.

Ariadne wasn't exactly sure how she came to be striding rapidly down the palm-tree-lined street toward the pool. She only knew she'd had to escape before she really blew. Anger and claustrophobia were an explosive combination

By the time she caught sight of Fay's floppy blue straw hat and distinguished Shanna's squeals of delight from those of another child, Ariadne had calmed down enough to despise the fact that she'd run away rather than stay and demand answers. She consoled herself with the thought that she probably wouldn't have gotten any. George Allandale had been evading direct questions all along. Just as Clay did.

Hot and sweaty again, Ariadne almost wished she had a swimsuit of her own. More than that, though, she wished she could hide her agitation. Fay was sure to know that something had gotten her stirred up. Her twin was nothing if not perceptive.

Fay took one look and knew who was to blame. "Poppa's a horrible man, Ari," she said. "He always has been."

Ariadne stared at her sister for a long moment, then blurted, "Thank goodness you feel that way, too!"

Intense relief was immediately followed by abject embarrassment. "I shouldn't have said that. You love him. He raised you."

"I do love my grandfather, but it's in spite of his manipulative ways, not because of them." She patted the deck chair next to her own. "Sit. Calm down. Deep breaths help."

"I usually count to ten."

"Does it work?"

"Not with George Allandale."

"Mommy! Look at me!" Shanna was splashing happily with another girl near her own age.

For a while, the two sisters sat in silence, watching the innocent children play.

"I should go back home." Ariadne broached the subject tentatively. It felt like she was giving up, and she'd never been a quitter. "There doesn't seem much point in staying on here. You and Lila can always come visit us in Maine."

"But you planned a week."

"That was before I ran into a brick wall."

"Poppa?" Ariadne nodded. "Mother was a lot like

him, you know. More than either of them would ever admit. But she was always quick to forgive. Poppa holds a mean grudge.''

''All the more reason to stay out of his way.''

''How about a compromise?'' Fay suggested. ''Why not think of the rest of your visit as Shanna's vacation? Let her get to know Nana, and keep your distance from the General.''

Ariadne kicked off her shoes and leaned back in the deck chair. ''I suppose. I'm just not sure I trust him. There are some subjects I don't want him to bring up in Shanna's hearing. Her father. My father.''

''I can run interference.'' Fay made the offer with such eagerness that Ariadne finally caught on. It was her sister who wanted more time with Shanna.

''Two pluses. One minus,'' Ariadne mused. ''Shanna did take to her great-grandmother. And she flat-out loves her aunt Fay.''

Pleased, Fay's expression softened. ''I love her, too.''

''So, tell me how we're going to get through the rest of the week without me killing dear old Granddad.''

''I already have a plan for tomorrow. What if Nana and Poppa and I take Shanna to Busch Gardens? It isn't far. Just a day trip. She'll love it, and you can stay behind, take some time for yourself.'' She slanted a speculative glance in Ariadne's direction. ''Or you could spend the day with Clay, if you want to.''

Oh, I want to, she thought. *But does he?*

She reached for the sunscreen, suddenly feeling the heat. She grimaced. Her flushed skin wasn't entirely due to the sun. Thoughts of being alone with Clay were having their usual effect on her.

Could she depend on Fay to look out for Shanna?

That was what she should be considering. Her sister did tend to let their grandfather have his way. On the other hand, Ariadne knew her sister was capable of digging in her heels when it came to something that was important to her. She certainly hadn't rushed back to Connecticut to reconcile with Gary just because Allandale wanted her to.

"So? What do you say?" Fay looked heartbreakingly eager.

"She can go. After all, my original reason for coming to Florida still stands. I don't want to make the same mistake with my daughter that Gramps made with me. I can't decide for her how she feels about the members of her family."

"And you and Clay will have some time for yourselves," Fay added, looking smug. "Excellent."

Muttering something noncommittal under her breath, Ariadne closed her eyes and leaned back in the deck chair. As she'd concluded earlier, her twin was nothing if not perceptive. She felt another wave of heat wash over her as Fay began to hum a decidedly off-key rendition of "I'm in the Mood for Love."

"Bye, pumpkin. Have a good time." Ariadne waved, then closed the door after her departing daughter and leaned against it with a sigh of relief. She met Clay's amused gaze. "It's tiring trying to keep up with a four-year-old. I'm glad of a break."

"Is that why you've got that worried expression on your face?" He sipped his coffee and continued to watch her.

Ariadne pushed off from the door and helped herself to some coffee from the room-service cart. She supposed she did sound defensive. She wasn't used to letting Shanna go off with virtual strangers. "I hope Fay knows what she's getting into," she murmured.

"She'll do fine. So will Shanna. You heard how excited she was to be going with her nana."

"And I also noticed that she avoided looking at her great-grandfather. I think he scares her, Clay."

"I think he scares you."

Cradling her coffee cup, Ariadne wandered to the picture window and looked out over the perfectly landscaped golf course attached to their resort hotel. "It always scares me to realize I'm out of my element."

It wasn't just this place, it was everything—the Allandales, Clay. She shivered and clasped her arms about herself for comfort.

Suddenly he was standing right behind her, so close that she could smell the faint trace of his spicy aftershave. Ariadne kept her eyes on the golf course instead, trying to focus on a small caravan of golf carts just setting out from the clubhouse. Spice. Caravans. Palm trees. Decidedly erotic images formed in her mind.

Shifting uncomfortably, she tried to keep Clay from noticing her flushed face. With everything else going on in her life right now, she didn't have any time to be interested in the opposite sex. It was absurd that every time she and Clay Franklin were in a room alone together, her imagination should take flight.

"You're on vacation, Ari," he said. "Relax."

"It's Shanna's vacation." She turned but managed to slide sideways at the same time. He was entirely too close for her peace of mind.

"She's going to have a great day." His eyes twinkled, as if he knew how nervous he was making her.

"Is Busch Gardens like Walt Disney World?" she

blurted, desperate to keep him talking. If he took another step toward her he'd be near enough to touch.

"It's smaller. Good thing, too. As it is, George and Lila will wear themselves out keeping up with Shanna."

Moving as cautiously as he would with a wounded animal, he relieved her of her now-empty coffee cup, placing it on a nearby end table, then took both her hands in his. "Here's the thing, Ari. While the little kid is taking a day to play, I think the big kids should take one, too. What do you say? No talk about family. No worrying about the future. No trying to figure out anyone's personality quirks. Just fun. Want to give it a try?"

What she wanted were his warm, hard hands moving up her arms, over her shoulders, down to—

Ariadne reined in her wayward thoughts, but it was too late. An answering flash of desire appeared in his eyes. For a breathless moment neither of them spoke. Then she swallowed and asked, "What did you have in mind?"

He cleared his throat. "A tour of the town. We can go shopping for sponges." One of his thumbs moved slowly, erotically, over the back of her hand.

Blinking, Ariadne struggled for comprehension, then gave up. "What?"

The wicked glint in his eyes told her he knew what was distracting her, but he patiently explained. "Tarpon Springs is famous for its sponges. They dive for them. If it appeals to you, we can take a tour of the docks and the dive boats. I'll buy you a sponge to take home as a souvenir."

Sponges called to mind baths. No—showers. And decadent images that brought heat rushing into her cheeks. When Clay abruptly released her, her first thought was that he knew what she was thinking and was shocked by it. She'd shocked herself with her brief fantasy, in which she'd behaved in an incredibly brazen way with a broad-shouldered, light-haired man who looked a lot like she imagined Clay would...if he weren't wearing any clothes.

"It's up to you, Ari. Tour the town or stay here."

Cautiously she met his gaze. He wasn't disgusted with her at all. In fact, he had that deceptively boyish grin on his face, the one she found so irresistible.

"Tour," she said quickly.

Chapter Nine

They spent the morning at the docks, and then went to a nearby Greek restaurant for a quiet lunch. It wasn't until Ariadne paused in the act of sampling a bite from Clay's meal, that she realized how well his plan had worked. She felt the most relaxed she'd been in days. And happy. Content. For the past few hours, she'd just been…herself again.

"I think I may have gotten through my identity crisis," she murmured.

Clay glanced at his watch. "Well, we've set a new record. Three solid hours without mentioning your family."

"I'm not talking about them now," she said quickly. "At least not directly. This is about me. And you. I owe you an apology."

A warm, comforting hand covered hers on the table. "I'm listening," he said.

"I wasn't very nice to you at first," she conceded.

"Understandable."

"Still, I want you to know now that I'm glad I found out the truth. I'm coming to grips with my situation. I may not like everything I've learned about my new family, but at least now that I know something of what happened in the past, I feel as if I can go forward and deal with the present. And the future."

Clay started to interrupt, but she rushed on. "It's obvious that Shanna and her great-grandmother have already formed a special bond. It still seems odd to me to have a twin, but Fay and I are comfortable with each other. I suspect it will be like having a very close friend for the rest of my life."

"I know Fay feels the same way." Clay looked as if he wanted to say more, but instead he shook his head and fell silent. Ariadne's elation dimmed.

Viewed from across the small table, he appeared to be perfectly content to be here with her. All morning long he'd been charming, thoughtful, funny—in short, everything she admired in a man. That he was easy on the eyes as well was a bonus. But they weren't on a date and they had no romantic future. She had to remember that.

The truth was that they had been thrown together temporarily and soon would go their separate ways again. If he ended up involved with anyone, it would be her sister, not her. And since Fay didn't seem to want him, he'd probably end up as alone as Ariadne was herself.

"Why the frown?" he asked.

Reluctant to tell him the precise truth, not certain she could explain what she was feeling anyway, she shrugged. "There are still a few things that bother me."

"Can you be more specific?"

Ariadne sighed. She accepted that she'd driven happiness away by wanting more than she could have. That being the case, since she did have questions, she decided she might as well voice them.

"I can't seem to shake the feeling that George Allandale is...hiding something."

She'd been wondering, ever since her quarrel with Allandale, if the dark hints in Gramps's letter might not have been exaggerations, after all. She couldn't put her finger on the reason why she felt so strongly about this, but there was definitely a piece or two missing from the jigsaw puzzle.

Clay's reaction to her comment was a hard, suspicious look that made Ariadne uneasy. She couldn't fathom the sudden change in him, but she felt a decided increase in the tension between them. She was aware, too, of a sense of loss. Had that earlier feeling of closeness been no more than an illusion?

Clay continued to stare at Ari until she dropped her gaze. He watched her toy nervously with the few morsels of food left on her plate and wondered how much she really knew. Had she found out how much the Allandales were worth? Was that why she'd put up with so much guff from George? Was that the real reason she'd let her daughter go with them today? What mercenary schemes was she dreaming up? And where did he fit into them?

Where *did* he fit in?

Giving Ari another probing look, he felt his doubts recede. Maybe he'd jumped to conclusions. Hell, he'd never been able to stay objective around her. Neither cynicism nor skepticism survived long when he was in her presence. He couldn't think of any other person in the world who could disarm him so easily.

Putting suspicion firmly aside, he saw what was real sitting right across the table from him. Ari looked troubled. She chewed her lower lip for a moment, then seemed to come to a decision. Her chin came up. Her gaze collided with his. There was nothing more sinister than deep concern in her dark eyes.

"What did George Allandale do before he retired?"

Still wary enough to edit his reply, Clay opted for a general answer. "He was a businessman. An entrepreneur." He still was. George's retirement had only meant he didn't go into the office every day anymore. Now, he worked at home. It was probably driving him nuts to have to make do in his temporary abode with only a laptop computer.

"Entrepreneur?" She wrinkled her nose. "That could mean anything."

While she mulled over his words, she began to gnaw her lip again. Clay wanted to reach across the table and stop her before she did any damage. He had his own plans for those lips.

"He had some dealings with the hotel business." As in owning at least seven of them, Clay thought.

Ari lifted pleading brown eyes to his and finally blurted out her real question. "I have to know. Was he involved in anything illegal? Organized crime or—?"

"Of course not!" He was genuinely shocked. George's business practices might tend toward the cut-throat, but he'd always stayed on the right side of the law.

"Thank goodness."

"Where on earth did you get a crazy idea like that?"

"I couldn't think of anything else that explained the discrepancies. They don't fit in at Hilltop Heights. And some people we talked to at the pool didn't even know who they were. And in his letter, Gramps implied—" She broke off, embarrassed, then added, defensively, "It wasn't *that* illogical to think they might be...well, hiding out."

"And I thought Fay had an overactive imagination!"

"Don't you dare laugh at me, Clay Franklin! There is something very odd going on here. I'm not entirely wrong to be suspicious."

"Why did you let Shanna go with them today if you really thought George might be a crook?"

"I knew Fay would take good care of her." She stabbed the last bit of food on her plate and popped it into her mouth.

"You don't know her any better than you do them."

"But I do. Somehow." Ari looked bewildered for a moment, then shrugged. "She's my twin."

"Haven't you ever heard of the evil twin?" Clay teased.

The mood between them lightened with the sound of her laughter. "Oh, come on, Clay. That's the stuff of fiction, not real life. And besides, I trust you, and you've been singing Fay's praises since we met."

"And George Allandale?"

"Well, I guess I knew that he couldn't be completely awful. In spite of the way he treats her, Fay loves him. And then there's Rover. Cats are excellent judges of character."

He knew he ought to let the matter drop, but the insight he was gaining into Ari's thinking was too fascinating. He had to have been crazy earlier to doubt her motives. She was everything he'd thought she was, and more. All of Fay's good qualities plus an abundance of her own. An altogether appealing combination.

And she deserved to know the truth.

"George and Lila moved just before you arrived. They didn't want you to see their real home. It's...very different from the one in Hilltop Heights."

Before he could finish his explanation, her eyes widened in amazed comprehension. "Of course. Pride. They were embarrassed."

Oblivious to his astonishment, giving him no chance to correct her, Ari rushed into her own explanation of the Allandales' deception.

"I know how hard it is for retired people to make ends meet. What a sweet thing to do, renting that place, furnished, because they were ashamed to have me see how they really live. It's just like that old Bette Davis movie, the one where she's a Manhattan bag lady and pretends to be rich when she finally meets her daughter. Can they afford a gesture like that?"

"They can afford Hilltop Heights." She was dead wrong, but Clay couldn't help loving the way her mind worked.

"I'd hate to think they had to eat cat food or something in order to—"

"Ari! Enough! George feeds Rover ground round."

Her compassion, misplaced though it was, spoke volumes about her true nature. That she could still be so concerned after all the nasty remarks George had made reminded Clay just how special she really was. Even more than her physical appearance, her open honesty drew him to her.

"Are you sure? I thought from the first that they didn't seem comfortable there. That they didn't quite fit into their surroundings. But I hate to think of them someplace worse.''

He only half listened as she continued to muse aloud, distracted by thoughts of the two of them fitting into surroundings of their own. Back at their hotel suite, for example. He knew exactly how he wanted to spend the rest of this day and it did not include further explanations of George Allandale's chicanery.

The sheer selfishness of his rationale gave Clay pause. He didn't trouble to hide his motives from himself. It wasn't any altruistic sense of justice that was prompting him to keep his silence. It was his desire not to turn Ari against him, his desire to take her to bed…his desire to keep her in his life.

Impossible.

He couldn't be thinking of any lasting relationship with Ariadne Palmer. He didn't go in for long-term liaisons. He told himself firmly that he was contemplating an affair, nothing more. She already knew the score on one count. Early on, he'd come right out and told her that he wasn't interested in marriage and family.

Tell her the rest, his conscience urged.

It might be wise to clear the air between them before they became intimate, so that there would be no recriminations, no misunderstandings. He didn't want her to end up feeling he'd betrayed her. On the other hand, he could kiss any romantic plans for this afternoon goodbye the moment he broke his promise to George.

''Clay?'' She was frowning again. ''There's something else that's odd.''

''What's that?''

''Every once in a while something in George Allandale's attitude reminds me of Emmaline Comfort,

Brad's mother. He seems to…well, look down his nose at me, just the way she always does when we meet in a store or on the street.'' Hands spread wide in confusion, unable to find the words to describe her impressions any more clearly, Ari waited for Clay to explain away her observation.

First Bette Davis. Now Emmaline Comfort.

The time had come, he decided as the waiter arrived to take their dessert order, to tell Ari everything. Since that would also involve telling her that her father had accepted a bribe from George, he couldn't just blurt it all out. He had to lead up to it.

''Let's wait until we're back in the suite,'' he suggested. ''I don't want anyone to overhear what I have to say.'' The Allandales had friends everywhere in Tarpon Springs. Now that he thought about it, he realized that one of Lila's Greek cousins owned this restaurant.

But an hour later, back in the privacy of their suite, when Clay indicated he was ready to talk, Ari surprised him yet again.

''No,'' she said in a thoughtful voice.

''What?''

''I don't want to talk anymore today,'' she said firmly. ''Nor do I want to see that serious look back on your face.''

It hadn't been there during dessert. They'd managed to relax again, to flirt, to pretend that they were on the brink of romance. Maybe it hadn't all been pretense. The way Ari was looking at him now suggested he wasn't the only one who'd been turned on by proximity on the taxi ride back to the hotel. He'd had a hard time keeping his hands to himself.

''We have a few hours left before Shanna comes back,'' she whispered. ''I want them to be special.''

"Have you been reading my mind?" He felt his expression soften and his heart speed up. *She* was special. He'd known that from the first, but he'd never realized until this moment just how much he could want to make her happy, to please her and pleasure her.

Dipping his head, he gently kissed her lips.

Her response was everything he'd hoped for and more. Her mouth was soft, welcoming. She tasted as sweet as the chocolate and whipped cream she'd had for dessert.

"Are you sure?" The moment he asked, he could have kicked himself for planting any doubts in her mind. The old, cynical Clay wouldn't have given her the chance to change her mind.

"I'm sure. I've abandoned common sense and I don't even care."

While scattering gentle kisses over his jaw and neck, Ari added, "On the ride back to the hotel from the restaurant I realized that after I go home I may never see you again."

"You can come to Hartford," he heard himself offer as he nibbled one small, perfect ear.

"It wouldn't be the same."

Suddenly uneasy, he pulled away from her—far enough to be able to see her eyes.

"I'm not asking for anything but today," Ari said. "I know I can't change who we are. But if you were any other man, I'd never have been attracted to you in the first place. If all I can have is one afternoon with you, then I want to enjoy every second of it."

He was ready to swear she was telling him the truth, but under his intense scrutiny she faltered. A flicker of doubt surfaced in those dark, expressive eyes. Clay bit back a groan. Holding her gently, he caught her chin with his fingertips to keep her from looking away. She'd embarrassed herself with her own boldness. He could see that. He thought he saw much more.

"Are you sure you won't have any regrets?"

"There is one thing. A question. I guess I have to know. First."

Not now!

His eyes closed briefly, but he nodded. "Ask."

"I need to know that I'm not just a...substitute."

He'd been dreading another question about George Allandale. For a moment he stared at her, uncomprehending. She had the same expectant look on her face that Shanna often wore, the same need for reassurance. "There is no one like you, Ari." Certainly not Barbara. Had someone told Ari about her? "There will be no woman but you in bed with me."

"Not even Fay?" she blurted. "If it's really Fay you want...if I'm second choice...a substitute for the one who got away...I can't handle that, Clay. I'm sorry, but that's one thing I just can't deal with."

Relief coursed through him. Fay? She thought he had the hots for her sister? Hugging her tightly to him, Clay rained kisses on Ari's face.

"I've never imagined Fay naked," he said gruffly, "and I've never dreamed about having her in my bed. But you, Ariadne Palmer, have been there since we met. Every night. In bed with me and with me in a dozen more erotic locales besides. It's damn near driven me crazy wanting you."

"Oh, Clay."

That seemed to be all she wanted to know, the only reassurance she needed. She didn't ask for promises, for commitment. Only that he wanted her for herself.

And he did. God help him.

And not just for one afternoon.

He put that radical thought aside to think about later. He couldn't put how he felt into words. Not yet. He was less cynical than he'd been before he met her, but he was not about to declare he was in love with anyone, not even Ari. The last time he'd said those words, he lived to regret them.

He couldn't tell her how he felt. But he could show her.

Ariadne's senses reeled. Lost in a maelstrom of erotic pleasure, she scarcely noticed that they'd moved from the living room to the bedroom he'd been using, or that her clothes were being shifted, lifted to give him access. She was aware only of the delightful sensations of warm hands on bare skin. Her bare skin. His wonderful, wicked hands.

Her focus centered wholly on Clay, on the textures and scents of the man who was about to become her lover. His shirt was a barrier to her pleasure. Awkward in her haste, she jerked at it, trying to get it off. He helped her, finally managing to strip it away to reveal a hard, tanned chest covered with a light dusting of golden hair. She bent her head and touched her mouth against his breastbone and found him salty to the taste.

Nostrils flaring, he lifted her into his arms and carried her the few remaining steps to the bed. Suddenly shyness overwhelmed her. "I haven't had much practice at this."

"Practice?" A slow smile transformed his face. An irreverent twinkle appeared in his eyes. "You mean as in piano lessons?"

"Don't tease."

He dipped his head toward her once more, capturing her lips, but she was still tense. It had been a long time.

The power of her attraction to Clay had made her forget just how awkward things had gotten those few times with Brad. She'd never had any desire to repeat the experience until now.

"Relax, Ari. You aren't performing for an audience here."

The kisses continued, slowly, then became more intense, deeper. She began to melt again. He shifted his focus, nipping at her earlobes, sipping at her lips, moving lower to caress her breasts. As he removed more of her clothing, he soothed her with words and touches. "We're going to take this slowly," he promised. "No sixteenth notes."

That made her smile and a moment later her hands were as busy as his, exploring hesitantly at first and then more boldly. "I do like...playing," she whispered.

"We're going to make beautiful music together, music that will please us both."

Words continued to woo her as his hands stroked and seduced. Soon she was out of control, rendered too weak to do anything but react to his gentle caresses.

"Easy rhythms," he murmured. "Nice and slow and simple, like your favorite piece from that first-year piano book."

Warm, firm lips settled over hers, this time capturing both body and mind. On a rush of pure elation, she felt the kiss deepen. It was heaven to cling to him, weak and willing, to trust someone that much. And it was suddenly easy to be more aggressive herself, to greedily kiss him back. Her last remnants of uncertainty, of nervousness, evaporated.

Excitement curled through her body as she explored the dark, secret recesses of his mouth with her tongue.

When his fingertips brushed her breast again she flowed into him, filling his hand with her flesh. With infinite slowness, his hand moved again, divesting her of a soft cotton camisole. It was swept away as his mouth seared a downward path, moist and hot, trailing a line of fire over chin and neck and collarbone until at last his lips began to suckle.

Ariadne gasped with pleasure. Desire exploded within her, heating steadily as it coursed through her veins. She arched toward him, her arms circling his neck, her fingers twining in his soft hair.

"Perfect," he whispered huskily. "I can't think of anything more splendid than to go on kissing you, loving you. Make love with me, Ari."

Her eyes drifted closed as she whispered her consent one last time. Then her whole being became centered on the gentle tugging of his lips. He kissed and caressed each breast, bringing one, then the other, to aching fullness. Her searching hands wove patterns on his back. She needed the feel of his bare flesh against her own.

Simmering heat coiled deliciously through her body as his lips returned to hers. Sparks shot through her veins. His hands slipped down along her body, stripping away one last bit of clothing and creating new conflagrations wherever they touched. She closed her eyes as rational thought fled. Pressing herself against him, Ariadne knew nothing but the feel of his hands, his mouth, his breath, heard nothing but his soft voice, murmuring encouragement. She was only peripherally aware that his clothing had followed hers to the floor and he'd taken a moment to don protection.

"Now," he whispered.

Eyes wide open, she watched his face, seeing his joy,

his almost-painful pleasure as he completed their union with a powerful surge.

Her moan was low and delighted. Nothing had ever felt this good, this right. And then, as if they had been doing it all their lives, they began to move together.

He stroked her until she burned with a fever both rare and glorious. She couldn't think, couldn't speak. And then she was engulfed in an explosion of heat as powerful as an erupting volcano. Ecstasy swept them both far away.

Limp in the aftermath of such exquisite lovemaking, they clung to each other, shifting their positions on the bed only so that Ariadne could pillow her head against his chest. Ariadne stared at his chin, his lips, a secret smile curving her mouth.

She had pleased him. She didn't need to hear him say it. She knew.

"Exceptional performance," he whispered close to her ear. "Brava, Ari." His chest moved as he spoke and she felt as well as heard the rumble of his deep, resonant chuckle.

"I never understood till now," Ariadne murmured.

"Understood what?" He shifted so that they were lying face-to-face, and he stroked her cheek, then tucked a stray strand of hair behind her ear.

Ariadne felt the embers kindle again. Amazing.

"What all the shouting was about," she answered. It was really quite remarkable that she could still be...tingling this way.

Clay gave her an odd look. "You never had an orgasm before? Is that what you're telling me?"

Ariadne felt color rush into her face at his bluntness. Why had she volunteered something so personal? But she'd let the information slip. There was no point now in denying it.

"I've only made love with one other man, and Brad never... You're the first to—" She stumbled to an abrupt stop, bemused by the pleased expression on his face.

Clay didn't know why her shy confession affected him so strongly, but he wasn't about to waste time on meditation. He tugged her closer, so that she could feel him from her chest to her toes. Her eyes widened.

"Maybe the big kids could...play just a little while longer?" he suggested.

"What did you have in mind?" A delightful pinkness rushed into her cheeks. "My, ah, encore had a lot of sixteenth notes."

"We don't want to rush," he told her. "But I wouldn't mind some water music. I've been wondering if those Tarpon Springs sponges live up to their billing."

Clay worried that he was expecting too much. She was inexperienced. Then he saw the sparkle replace the shyness in her eyes. With him, for him, she was ready to try anything.

"The shower in this room is big enough for two," he said.

Like two naughty children, they left the bed and headed for the luxuriously appointed bath. They stopped to embrace, to kiss, and he had to reach around her into the shower stall to turn on the water. He was barely able to concentrate on what he was doing long enough to get the temperature right. He'd never been this frantic for a woman. He felt as if he'd die if he didn't have her again soon. His lips locked on hers, his hands left the faucet to cup her breasts.

"Perfect," he murmured.

"Sponge them for me?" she teased, then looked surprised and pleased at her own boldness.

A small measure of Clay's sanity returned. "We left the sponge in the other room." Reluctantly he stepped away from her, letting his eyes feast on her as he backed toward the door. "Don't move. Don't think. I'll be right back."

It took less than a minute to retrieve the gigantic brown sponge from the shopping bag, and in spite of his need for her, or perhaps because of it, he paused a moment longer to collect another small foil packet.

The cynic surfaced, reminding him that she'd been accused of trying to spring the baby trap on Brad Comfort. He didn't believe it. Worse, he realized that the thought of Ariadne Palmer having his baby did not appall him as it should have. He stared down at the condom in his hand and shook his head to clear it.

"Clay?"

She was waiting for him. Naked. Willing. His hand closed around the packet and he went to her.

Ari had already stepped into the shower. Water glistened on her flushed skin, drawing his eyes to the places where it lingered. The tips of her breasts. The end of her nose. The indentation at her navel.

He was lost from that moment. He stepped under the warm stream of water and took her into his arms and into his heart. "Ari," he breathed as his lips hungrily captured hers.

It was magic, she thought. Enchantment. Her earlier fantasy come true with no room for embarrassment.

The sponge moved over her until her skin tingled. Or maybe that was the effect of Clay's mouth, his fingertips as he teased her into a frenzy of desire. She felt utterly boneless by the time he bent his knees, lifted her slightly and slid inside her. For a moment, time stopped. Ariadne's eyes met his lambent gaze as he began to move. Amazingly, almost at once, she was caught up in the sensations of her release, the mad, indescribable ecstasy of what the right man could make a woman feel.

He felt her clenching around him, and that triggered the culmination he'd been holding back. Clay surrendered to the firestorm, giving up the last vestige of his control. She made him lose himself in her. That should have terrified him. Instead, he felt only a blissful sense that, at last, he was complete. He was quietly certain that no other woman would ever affect him in quite this same way.

"I guess we hit a few sixteenth notes, after all," he whispered. He felt her smile against his cheek.

"Time to shift to dry land," he whispered when the water began to cool.

"Mmm." Ari sounded utterly content.

By the time they'd finished drying each other off with the big, fluffy towels the hotel provided for its guests, he was aroused all over again. "You're addictive," he accused.

"You, too." Snuggling closer, Ariadne thought about what they'd just shared. Still astonished, still delighted, she wasn't sorry she'd given in to passion.

"You know, they say practice makes perfect." He was steering her back into the bedroom, back toward the bed. Sunlight fell on the rumpled sheets, slanting in through the window.

With a sense of shock, she realized they'd been making love all afternoon. She didn't want their time together to end, but there was no denying that it must.

Soon. "It's getting late," she said, a quiver in her voice.

"One afternoon isn't enough."

"Are you asking me to have an affair with you?" A terrible coldness crept into her soul when he hesitated.

"I...I don't know what I'm asking, except to be with you like this again. Soon."

They were still touching. Still naked. Suddenly Ariadne shivered. No matter how blissful their lovemaking had been, the word *affair* conjured up unpleasant images. Stolen afternoons in hotel rooms. Secrecy.

Sensing the change in her, Clay tensed. "Ari, I'm not letting you go."

Unable to meet his eyes, overwhelmed by a feeling of panic, she pulled free of his embrace. "I have to get dressed. I don't want Shanna to find me like this."

She bolted, devastated by the knowledge that she would have to put an end to their sexual relationship. She didn't want to, but she couldn't see that she had any choice. Her daughter's welfare had to come first. An affair was out of the question and Clay Franklin had told her in the beginning that he was not the marrying kind.

Good thing, she told herself. She didn't want to change her life. She wouldn't marry him even if he asked. Why, she'd wither and die if she had to play the role of corporate wife.

Clay waited until she closed the door behind her before he dressed. Then he went out and sat on the living room sofa to wait for her. When she chose to sit on the love seat opposite, instead of beside him, he was certain he wasn't going to like what she said next.

It was a good thing, he decided, that he hadn't risked

revealing his true feelings for her. He could see it now. He'd have told her that he loved her and she'd have behaved just as Barbara had. Did Ari already have a prenuptial contract drawn up, he wondered cynically, or did she believe in making more spontaneous demands?

No. That was wrong. Whatever was troubling Ari, it didn't have anything to do with using him. He was the one who'd deceived her, a fact it was going to be even harder to deal with now that they'd been lovers.

"Ladies first," he offered, taking the coward's way out.

She stumbled over her words, her agitation obvious. "Having an affair would be bad for Shanna," she said. "I care for you, Clay, but I can't let this...affair continue. And I understand that you don't want more than a casual relationship. I'd never ask it of you."

Listening to his own words, his own philosophy, coming back at him ironically made Clay want to argue the other side of the case. But when she faltered into silence and sat waiting anxiously for him to speak, he hesitated. He kept forgetting, or perhaps repressing, the one thing that really stood in the way of any relationship between them. He'd misled her. He'd never lied, except to himself, but he'd come damn close to it with Ari.

Clay cleared his throat. He had to be completely honest with her now and hope that she would understand why he'd gone along with her grandfather's scheme. If she could find it in her heart to forgive him, they might still have a future together.

He didn't let himself dwell on what, exactly, he wanted that future to entail. Not yet. He only knew that he wanted both Ari and her daughter to have a permanent place in his life.

He opened his mouth, prepared to speak his piece.

A tremendous pounding cut him off.

"Ari? Clay?" There was an edge in Fay's voice that had Ari exchanging a quick, worried look with Clay, then rushing toward the door to let her sister in.

One concern was immediately dispelled. Shanna was with her aunt and didn't look as if she was ill or upset. Fay was another matter.

"Look after Shanna," Fay called to him over her shoulder as she hustled Ari into the other room.

Damn. Something had happened at that amusement park. He hadn't seen Fay this visibly shaken, or this furious, in years.

"Mommy," Shanna called, starting after them.

Double damn.

"Hold on, little buddy. Your mother will be back in a minute."

Shanna stopped, turned and gave him a suspicious look. "I want Mommy, now."

Clay tried an engaging smile, though the last thing he felt like doing was distracting a four-year-old. Whatever was going down, Ari wouldn't want her daughter in the middle of it. He didn't, either. "Won't I do?" he asked Shanna.

"I want to tell *Mommy* about the water slide."

"I bet that was fun." *I'm dying here,* Clay thought, but he kept gamely on. "Were you scared?"

Sticking out her chin, she declared, "I'm brave."

Although it was obvious Shanna still wanted to tell her mother all about her day, she began to respond to his interest. It was touch and go for a moment longer. He knew Fay well enough to be certain she hadn't let

Shanna guess how upset she was. Still, by now, the little girl must have suspected something was wrong. She looked back over her shoulder once more as she came away from the door.

"Mommy and Aunt Fay will come out soon," Clay assured her. "They just need to talk to each other in private for a few minutes. So, Shanna, did you go on any other rides?"

"No," she said sulkily. "We looked at animals. And we had lunch. And we went and watched some people in funny costumes do a dance. And then Aunt Fay yelled at that man."

"At your great-grandfather?"

"He's not Bumpa."

"No, I know that. He's your other great-grandfather."

Shanna's lower lip crept forward into a pouty expression and she crossed her arms in front of her chest. "I'm not gonna go live with him."

What the hell was George up to now? Clay rejected the idea of asking Shanna more questions. She was just a child and he didn't want to upset her. Even though she'd obviously already sensed the tension between the adults, he didn't want to make matters worse.

"Why don't I get your mother?" he suggested. "Will you wait here while I see if she's through with your aunt Fay?"

He'd had little experience with children. Shanna looked like she was about to cloud up and rain and he didn't have a clue what to do if that happened. But even tired and weepy as she was, the little girl apparently still trusted him. She planted herself on a footstool and watched his every move as he made his way to the bedroom door.

It loomed before him. Barrier or gateway? The lady or the tiger? Some knight in shining armor he was! Clay had the distinct impression that he'd just had his horse shot out from under him.

Chapter Ten

"This is the last straw," Ari was saying when Clay opened the door. Her voice was low, to keep Shanna from hearing her, but fury suffused every syllable. "Absolutely the last straw!"

"What is, Ari?" Clay was surprised when the question made it past the lump in his throat.

It was Fay who answered. "Poppa says he and Nana are going to try to take Shanna away from Ari, so they can bring her up 'properly.'"

No wonder Ari looked shell-shocked.

"He even proposed it to Shanna," she raged. "He said, 'Would you like to come and live with us, little girl? We have a great big house, with lots of room for someone your size. Just ask your aunt Fay. She grew up there.'"

"Big house?" Ari echoed. "What big house?" Horror mixed with disbelief on her face.

Driven by a powerful anger of her own, Fay had forgotten that her sister did not yet know that the Allandales were wealthier than the Comforts ever dreamed of being.

"They're rich, Ari," she blurted. Clay didn't try to stop her. What was the use? It would all come out now. "Poppa and Nana aren't quite billionaires, but they are extremely well-off." Fay's voice began to shake as the bitterness in it grew. "Poppa was so afraid you'd turn out to be a gold digger that he moved into that retirement community to deceive you. He wanted you to think he didn't have anything you'd want, so you'd go away and leave my inheritance intact. It was all for my sake, you see. Until he met Shanna."

Ari sat down abruptly on the edge of the bed, as if her legs could no longer support her. Clay knew the moment understanding hit her, the moment his chances of salvaging their relationship plummeted. Her shoulders slumped and she took care from then on that her gaze never wandered anywhere near him.

"Why did you go along with him?" Ari asked her twin.

"Habit." Fay sounded disgusted with herself. "It's always been easier to do what he wants than to quarrel. But he went too far this time. He's convinced that you won't do, but he wants your daughter. He wants to give her things, raise her as he raised our mother, as he raised me. Well, let me tell you, being brought up in that big house by George Allandale is not all that good for a child." Fay's voice suddenly escalated into a wail. "I wanted my mother, no matter what kind of life she was leading."

"He's not getting my daughter."

Fay rushed to her sister's side and hugged her tightly, just what Clay wished he could do.

"I knew as soon as I met you that you weren't after the Allandale money," Fay declared. "I'd have told you everything right away if he hadn't made us promise not to."

Tears streamed down Fay's face as she embraced her sister again. Ari hugged her back, but her eyes were dry. Over Fay's shoulder, she finally looked for Clay and found him still frozen in the doorway.

"You knew all along," she accused. "You knew and you went along with his lies."

No excuse sufficed, no explanation was good enough to make up for the disillusionment he saw in her expression. "Yes, I knew all along," he admitted. And almost from the beginning he'd known how the discovery of their deception would affect her.

She had forgiven Edward Palmer for keeping secrets from her, even for lying to her, but Clay wasn't at all sure she could ever forgive him.

Their blissful afternoon of lovemaking must now appear to be the ultimate betrayal.

Chest tight, eyes burning with unshed tears, Ariadne buried her head on her sister's shoulder. Never in her life had she felt so devastated. Not even her discovery that Gramps had lied had been this painful.

Because I love him, she thought. *Oh, damn. I went and fell in love with him.*

For just a moment, before Fay's timely arrival, she'd thought there might be a chance that he loved her, too. There had been something in the way Clay looked at her, with such regret and so much tenderness that she'd dared to hope he did want more than a casual affair.

The more fool she! It would never have worked anyway. They were too different.

"Mommy, aren't you ever going to come out?"

The sight of Shanna at Clay's side sent a wave of guilt washing over Ariadne. How could she have been so selfish? She'd wanted Clay, wanted what had happened between them this afternoon, and to have it, she'd sent her daughter right into George Allandale's clutches. She'd risked her precious child's welfare for the chance to be wanton. Decadent. Self-indulgent.

Through a blur of tears she saw Clay trying to reason with Shanna, to convince her to go back out into the living room. The sight unnerved her.

"Come here, pumpkin," she called, hastily wiping her eyes. Shanna was her first priority. She would not forget that again.

Satisfied that she had her mother's full attention at last, Shanna began to chatter happily about the many sights and sounds of Busch Gardens. If she'd been upset by the strange behavior of the adults around her, it no longer troubled her, not with Mommy holding her on her lap and cosseting her.

Nearly half an hour passed before Ariadne got Shanna settled in front of the television set with a coloring book for backup. She accepted Fay's offer to keep an eye on the little girl, went into the bedroom she and Shanna had been sharing and closed the door behind her.

Ariadne thought she'd gotten herself under control, even though her heart felt as if it had been broken right in two, but all it took was a glimpse of Clay to send her reeling again. He'd been waiting to talk to her. When she came in, he rose from his perch on the edge of her bed and started toward her.

Evading him, she went to stand at the window, to stare as she had once before at the perfectly manicured, totally alien landscape. She didn't belong here. She never had.

Her own reflection looked back at her in the window, its expression tormented. Behind her, she could see Clay's familiar shape, though she couldn't make out his features. He seemed to be watching her, waiting for a sign of encouragement.

Pain lanced through her. The memory of their perfect afternoon together already haunted her and she had a feeling it would for a long time to come. She didn't dare dwell on any aspect of it now. She'd shatter into a million pieces if she did.

When his reflection moved toward her, she yielded to panic. "Stay where you are."

"Look at me, Ari."

Closing her eyes, she kept her back to him and shook her head. She heard a sigh of resignation, and a rustle of fabric that indicated movement, but he didn't sound any closer. "All right. Just listen, then. I should never have agreed to George's conditions. I meant to tell you everything today, before we...before we..."

"Hit the shower?" She spun around to glare at him.

"Falling back on sarcasm?" he asked, quirking a brow.

"You deceived me, Clay. Betrayed me." *Made me fall in love with you!*

Raking both hands through his hair, he looked as distraught as she felt, but she steeled herself not to feel any compassion for him. He was at fault. He'd brought this on himself.

"You have to understand how it looked at first," he said. "There was your father's history and the fact that the Comforts insisted you'd been after their money. And you appeared to be taking advantage of Laurie.''

After money? The absurdity of that might have amused her under other circumstances. Now it just increased her anger and confusion. Very little of this made sense. She fixed on the part of his explanation that made none at all.

"What do you mean, my father's history? What did he ever do that was so terrible?''

"He demanded money from George Allandale to divorce your mother.''

Another blow. Painful. Ariadne sucked in a breath and let it out. She tried counting to ten but at five she gave up. "I don't believe you.''

"It doesn't matter what you believe.'' Impatience made his voice harsh. "The fact is that George paid to get rid of an unsuitable son-in-law. When Duncan's report came in with Emmaline Comfort's charges that you were a gold digger, and that you'd latched on to Laurie for her money when Brad wouldn't marry you, what else was George to assume but that you were just like your father? When he couldn't talk Fay out of contacting you, he insisted we both agree to this deception as a way of testing you. He was afraid to let you find out how much money he had. He didn't want Fay to have to share her inheritance.''

The idea that someone would go to such lengths for any reason astonished Ariadne. "I don't want a share of anything,'' she protested.

"It made sense to him to be cautious, especially since he was dealing with such a large sum of money. Try to understand how—''

"Oh, I understand all right! George Allandale wanted to test me. Try put me on trial. And what about being innocent until proven guilty? And for that matter, why were you so sure George was telling the truth? What if he's lying about my father? Did you ask for proof? Evidence? Does he have a canceled check?''

"Your father was paid off in cash.''

"Hah! A likely story!''

"Ari—'' He took her arm. She shook him off. "Think, Ari. You're angry now, but don't be hasty. What reason would George have to lie about your father?''

Pacing, she put the width of the room between them. Think, he'd said. All right. What other explanation was there? "My grandmother Palmer was ill then,'' she said slowly. "She died before I was a year old. If my father took that money, it must have been to help his mother pay her medical bills.''

"We will probably never know exactly what happened in the past.'' Clay sounded skeptical. "What does it matter now, anyway? I'm concerned about the present and the future. About us.''

"It matters to me, and there *is* no us.''

"I was going to tell you. In fact,'' Clay said, catching her, lifting her chin with his finger until she looked at him, then holding her gaze with his own, "I was also going to tell you how I'd come to feel about you, Ari.''

"Oh, please! Not a declaration of love!''

As she broke free, she caught a glimpse of his face. If she hadn't known better, she'd have thought her sarcasm had wounded him.

"I've been in turmoil from the moment I first set eyes on you,'' he said irritably. "Why should things be any different now?''

"You thought I was a gold digger!''

"Yes."

"And now?"

She saw the flicker of doubt in his eyes and it infuriated her further. "How could you think... Why would you...? Damn it, Clay. You *know* me!"

She'd meant he ought to know her better than that by now, but the words came out all wrong. Vivid memories of just how well he knew her in the Biblical sense had her stuttering and stumbling. Waves of anger threatened to swamp her. Anger at herself as well as at Clay.

"You don't know me at all," she blurted.

"Yes, I can see that." Regret tinged his words. "For a while, Ari, I thought we might have something special between us. My mistake."

Stung, she fought tears. "We're too different. We always were. And you never did believe in me. Not really." That was what hurt so much. "It was so much easier to believe I was lying, wasn't it, Clay?" At last she could look at him directly, and she felt she was seeing him clearly for the first time. "You've lost the ability to believe in anyone."

"Ari—"

"No. I knew from the beginning it would never work."

"I thought it *worked* rather well." His gaze slid toward the open door to the bath, which was identical in design to the one in his room.

"That's just physical attraction, Clay. Get over it."

Why was she saying these things?

Every word she spoke made the rift between them wider. That was good, she told herself. She didn't want anything more to do with Clay Franklin. She wanted to drive him away.

For a moment, she thought she saw her own pain reflected in his eyes. Horrified at the thought that she might be destroying something that was real, something she wanted as badly as she wanted her next breath, Ariadne stared at him, willing him to come to her, to ask her to trust him, even though he'd failed to trust her.

Desperation gripped her. She prayed he didn't realize how easily he could change her mind. One more step in her direction would bring him close enough to take her into his arms. She'd be blurting out an apology for all the things she'd said in anger. She'd be confessing that she loved him.

Closing her eyes for a moment, Ariadne tried to regroup, to remember why it was so important to end this now. The sound of a childish giggle from the next room was just the reminder she needed.

"A person is not defined by her family or by the size of her bank account or by the lies others tell," she said primly. "I don't want anything more to do with any of you. Shanna and I can get along on our own, just as we did before you pushed your way into our lives."

That little speech, delivered in the calmest tone she was able to manage, seemed to make more of an impression on Clay than her earlier outbursts and accusations.

"We have unfinished business between us, but I can see you need to think things through." His hazel eyes gleamed with determination even as one hand strayed to the back of his neck and clenched, giving away the extent of his tension. "And I need to have a talk with George," he added grimly. "Something I should have done a long time ago."

Perplexed, still angry, Ariadne stood very still, wondering what was going on in his mind. There was something intimidating about Clay's stance. Even as that thought came to her, he moved, taking one short, aggressive step in her direction to seize her by the shoulders. Then his mouth was on hers as he kissed her with rough and devastating thoroughness.

Breathless, her thoughts scattered, she clutched his shoulders, not sure herself if she was trying to pull him closer or push him away. She had no chance to resolve the dilemma before Clay released her. Without another word, he turned his back on her and left the room.

Ariadne stared after him in dismay, her shaking fingers drifting up to touch tender lips. It might have been moments or aeons later before her mind began to function again. With a sob, she stumbled toward the closet, reaching blindly for her suitcases.

One bag was full, the other nearly so when Fay came to check on her. "What are you doing, Ari?"

"Protecting my emotional well-being. Where's Shanna?"

"She's busy doing a puzzle on the coffee table. Why are you packing?"

"Isn't it obvious? I'm going home."

"Don't you think you should wait until Clay comes back?"

"There's nothing left for us to say to each other." Seeing him again would be a mistake. She was weak where he was concerned. Even now she wanted to run after him to apologize.

"Ari?" Fay tried again. "Clay cares about you."

"Nice way to show it!" Whirling around to face her sister, Ariadne glared. "He lied to me."

"Poppa lied, not Clay."

"Clay went along with it."

"So did I."

"You warned me there was something you couldn't tell me. You wanted to tell me the truth. Clay lied."

"He didn't lie. If he'd broken his promise to Poppa, that would have been the lie. It was a stupid promise, but binding all the same, and Clay is an honorable man."

"You dropped hints. He could have done the same. If he really cared about me. If he believed in my innocence. But he didn't, did he? He always thought there was a possibility that I was as bad as Emmaline Comfort painted me."

"You're not being fair. You've obviously forgiven me for deceiving you. Why can't you forgive him? The only one who's really guilty here is our dear old grandfather."

Was she being unfair? Maybe she was, but it couldn't be helped. She had to protect herself. And Shanna. The only way she was going to fall out of love with Clay Franklin was to harden her heart.

"There was no reason for him to assume the worst," she said, her voice bitter. She pulled Shanna's shorts and T-shirts out of a dresser drawer and began to fold them.

Fay's hesitant words were spoken softly, but they riveted Ariadne's attention. "There *was* a reason. Is a reason. One that has nothing to do with the kind of woman you are." Fay took a deep breath, then blurted, "Her name is Barbara. Barbara Teasdale Franklin."

Shocked, Ariadne dropped the pair of socks she'd picked up. "His wife? He lied about that, too?"

"No!" Shaking her head, Fay looked thoroughly exasperated. "Stop jumping to conclusions. If nothing else, have a little faith in me. I wouldn't have been pushing you at a married man."

"Sorry."

In the time it took to retrieve Shanna's socks from the floor and deposit them in the open suitcase, Ariadne realized she had to know more.

"What did...Barbara do to him?"

"Clay is the one who should be telling you about her."

"Fay." That warning tone of voice, the same one which worked so well when Shanna misbehaved, had Ariadne's sister throwing up her hands in capitulation.

"Oh, all right. But keep in mind that even though Clay and I are close friends, I'm only guessing about some of this. As far as I know, he's never shared all the details with anyone."

"Let me guess—this woman was after his money?"

"Nothing so simple. Barbara wanted power. A partnership in the firm. Social connections. Clay's lucky he caught on in time, before he married her."

Frowning, Ariadne recited the list of names of Clay's law firm. "Franklin, Manley, Murphy, Franklin and Teasdale. But if she didn't marry Clay, how—"

"She worked for the firm and she and Clay were...close. Everyone expected they'd get married. Instead, they broke up. A few weeks later she came back from a conference in Las Vegas married to Clay's father."

Ariadne had to swallow before she could speak. "Well, that certainly goes a long way toward explaining his cynical attitude about love and marriage and women."

"He hasn't been quite so cynical lately," Fay pointed out.

"Don't start." Ariadne knew it would be far too easy to begin to hope again. "What you've told me about Barbara doesn't really change anything."

For a few silent moments, Fay stood watching her sister pack. Then she crossed to the bedside phone. "I'll call the airport," she offered.

Ten minutes later she relayed the news that their flight, direct to Boston, would leave Tampa in ninety minutes. She'd booked three seats. Ariadne clicked the locks on her luggage and gave her twin a long, hard look.

"What?" Fay sounded defensive. "I need to get back to my job anyway."

"And Gary?"

"Maybe."

"Because your grandfather wants you to reconcile?"

"Only in part." Fay reached for the toy bag, avoiding Ariadne's eyes as she stuffed in coloring books, Barbie clothes and Play-Doh. "I can't decide anything until I see Gary again, can I? I'll admit it's tempting to run away from troubles. I've done it often enough in the past. But they never get solved that way. Sometimes they just get more complicated."

"I am not running away from anything."

"Did I say you were? I thought I was talking about myself." Fay's innocent look was not convincing.

"I have a job to get back to, too," Ariadne reminded her. "A life. A good life. One without any man in it. No one at home can tell me what to do."

"Lucky you," Fay muttered.

Ariadne went to the door to check on Shanna. Her daughter had abandoned the puzzle for one of her dolls.

She was dancing it around the living room and singing to herself.

Satisfied, Ariadne made a last check of the drawers and closets. "I'm not going to change my mind about staying," she said, as much to convince herself as Fay. "I'm taking Shanna and returning to Maine. If Clay really thinks we have unfinished business, he knows where to find me."

The Allandales' real Florida house was less pretentious than the one in Connecticut—a simple, three-story stucco mansion on a quiet, tree-lined street. George betrayed only mild surprise when Clay stalked into his soundproof, air-conditioned office.

"Congratulations, George. You've succeeded in revealing Ariadne Palmer's true nature."

Even George couldn't miss sarcasm that heavy. "What are you talking about, boy?"

"I'm talking about this business of Shanna coming to live with you and Lila. About you trying to take a four-year-old child away from her mother." Crossing the room, Clay flattened his palms on the desk and leaned in. George's wary expression turned into a scowl.

"What's so bad about wanting a child to be brought up properly?" George stood. Clay straightened. Their gazes remained locked. "I'll pay Ariadne well to leave her daughter with me. Everyone will be better off."

"It's illegal to buy a child."

"Everything's for sale. How do you think we got Fay?"

"How do you think you lost Phyllis?" Disgusted, Clay turned away, his gaze roving over state-of-the-art office equipment without really seeing it. The man was insufferable. A control freak. "I thought there might be a child-custody threat from Brad Comfort," he muttered, "but I never imagined Ari would have to put up with that kind of harassment from her own grandfather."

As soon as the words were out, Clay regretted them. George was on them like a terrier on a postman's pant leg. "Comfort doesn't think she's a fit mother?"

Patience, Clay warned himself as he faced George once more. He'd come here to settle a few things, not to get into a shouting match. "Comfort has a wife who was curious about Shanna. Thanks to Duncan's questions. Thanks to your interference in Fay's original plan to contact her sister directly."

"I've done nothing but try to protect what's mine." George spoke with such conviction that Clay wondered if he was wasting his time. Talking sense into the man was like lecturing a stone wall.

"Ari wants no part of your money," he said, spacing each word for emphasis. "She insists, in fact, that she's going to make her own way in the world. She'll do it, too. She's managed just fine so far." When George said nothing, only sat there with an intractable expression on his hard face, Clay seriously considered cutting his losses and leaving. By the time he drove back through rush-hour traffic, Ari would have calmed down some. They'd be able to work things out.

"Damn fool girl would still be alive if she'd listened to me."

Startled, Clay needed a minute to figure out that George was talking about his daughter, Phyllis. He watched and listened in growing concern as George grumbled and muttered to himself, alternately blustering and sounding morose. He seemed oblivious to Clay's continued presence in his office.

A reluctant sympathy surfaced, overriding Clay's irritation. This was a George Allandale he'd never seen before. Old, embittered, afraid to let go of even the smallest bit of control—had he become that way because he'd lost the one person who'd mattered most to him? Or had he always been that way? Was that why he'd lost Phyllis to Mark Palmer in the first place? Did he blame himself for her wild ways? Did he regret, now that it was too late, that she'd died with the differences between them unreconciled?

"You can't control what happens to other people, George."

As if the words brought him suddenly back to himself, George stopped his restless movements and scowled at Clay. "I just wanted what was best for the girl."

From the tormented look on his face, memories were assaulting him. Bittersweet thoughts of his only child, the daughter he'd driven away by loving her too much.

"Mercenary bastard," he muttered.

Mark Palmer, Clay assumed. "Then why did you let him take Ari? Why didn't you just up the ante and keep both children?"

At first Clay didn't think George would answer, but slowly, painfully, words forced their way through lips tightly compressed against revealing any emotion. "He wanted one of them. Insisted. I made the best bargain I could and lived with it. It doesn't do any good to try to go back and fix things. Waste of time."

A confession of failure? George stood with his shoulders slumped, reinforcing the image. "What re-

ally came between Phyllis and Mark Palmer?'' Clay
dared ask. "You?''

"They were all wrong for each other.''

"Was that Phyllis's opinion? Or yours?''

"She agreed with me.''

"Did she? Or did you just keep after her until it was
easier for her to give in?''

"Damn it, boy! I did what I had to do.'' The old
George was back, prickly as a cactus. "Phyllis should
have been grateful.''

"I haven't been a boy for a long time, George.''

As George stalked back to his desk, resumed his
chair and got control of his formidable temper, Clay
felt as if he could read the old man's mind. George
was telling himself that intimidation worked best with
a cool head. But even though he was expecting a new
tactic, Clay was surprised by the weapon George chose.

"You're in love with Ariadne,'' he accused.

The impact of those words had as much force as a
roundhouse punch. Ari's grandfather was more perceptive than Clay had anticipated. He didn't have to say a
word aloud to confirm George's diagnosis, either, but
he suddenly needed to make his feelings crystal clear.
To both of them.

"I love Ariadne,'' he said. "If I can ever convince
her to forgive me for going along with your deceptions,
I'm going to ask her to marry me.''

"Why couldn't you have fallen for Fay?'' George
sounded thoroughly disgusted.

"Because she's not Ari.'' Strange as it seemed, that
simple statement said it all.

"Fay is my heir. Always will be. My only heir.''

"This may shock you, George, but your money has
nothing to do with what happens between Ari and me.''

Once more Clay leaned in close across the desk, but this time he spoke without sarcasm or anger. "If you want to spend time with Shanna in the future, you'll have to get used to the idea that money can't buy love."

"I'll have other great-grandchildren."

Unnerved, Clay kept his expression carefully noncommittal and his voice bland. He'd barely admitted to himself yet that he wanted to have children with Ari. "I'll need to talk to Ari about that, George. After we settle a few other things. We have a few matters to straighten out first."

To say the least.

She needed to be alone to think, to calm down. Or so he'd told himself at the time. Now he wondered. He'd made almost as many mistakes as George had in dealing with the women in his life.

Faced with the depth of his feelings for Ari, he was suddenly uncertain. Surely she must return his love. She wasn't the kind of woman who could give herself that completely in bed without making some emotional commitment.

"No," George said abruptly, startling Clay and commanding his full attention.

"No, what?" He braced himself. George apparently had one more trick up his sleeve.

"We don't need her or her daughter. Get Fay that divorce she wants. Marry her. Then you two can produce all the great-grandchildren Lila wants. We'll just forget this whole unfortunate incident ever happened."

Clay couldn't believe what he was hearing. He was beginning to wonder if George had a screw loose somewhere. Whatever sympathy he'd been feeling for the other man flew out the window when George opened the desk drawer and pulled out his checkbook.

"I'll pay your fees myself. I want her divorced and the two of you married within six months."

"Not a chance."

"How much do you want?"

Astonishment turned to fury. Clay's hands itched to reach across the desk and grab George by the throat. If ever anyone deserved to be throttled, it was George Allandale. To keep from doing something he'd regret, Clay kept his fists at his sides. His words came out cold and clipped.

"I'm not for sale, George. Have you forgotten I've got money of my own?"

"A man can always use more."

Disgusted, Clay turned to leave.

"Come back here. You work for me."

"I'm Fay's lawyer, not yours. And I won't be working for her much longer." The cynical mind-set of a divorce lawyer had gotten him into this mess. He already knew he was going to have to give some serious thought to making changes. If he expected to have a future with Ari he could not go on as he had been.

The drive back to the hotel seemed endless. Traffic on Route 19 was heavy. At least one accident slowed things further. Finally, though, he reached their suite.

The empty rooms mocked him. He could still smell the faint, lingering scent of her perfume, but as soon as he opened the door he knew Ari herself was gone. A prisoner of his racing thoughts, Clay struggled to cope with her desertion. He hadn't expected this. He didn't know how to handle it. Hell, he didn't even know how to explain it.

Ari had left him.

She'd given herself freely and then just walked away.

A note from Fay was propped up on the bar, telling him they were on their way to the airport and what flight they were taking. A quick glance at his watch told Clay it was already too late to catch them.

His first impulse was to go after her. To follow her back to Maine. To stay until he found a way to make things right. But although he searched the entire suite a second time, he found no message from Ari.

Disillusioned and disappointed, Clay reached desperately for all the old shields. He'd built his cynicism into a protective wall over the years, after Barbara had shown him what women were really like. Somehow Ari had gotten through it.

Disbelief slowly gave way to anger. Ari had deserted him. Betrayed him. Maybe he'd been wrong about her feelings for him, after all. He'd let down his guard. Had he been suckered? Again?

Pride now stood in the way of going after her, together with the certainty that he'd end up doing something totally irrational if he did—like blurting out that he loved her. Hell, he'd be begging her to marry him before he was through.

Thoroughly disgusted with himself, Clay collected his belongings and drove to the airport. The flight to Boston had left right on schedule. He'd never have been in time to catch it. He'd known that before he left the hotel, but hadn't quite been able to quell the tiny flicker of hope that there had been a delay.

Bitter regret gnawed at him, along with a sense of resignation. Ari had made her message crystal clear. She'd meant what she'd said. She didn't want anything more to do with any of them.

"Something else, sir?" the woman at the airline information desk asked. "Did you want to make a reservation on the next flight to Boston?"

"No," Clay told her. It took both hands to knead the knot of tension at the back of his neck. "Looks like my final destination is going to be Hartford."

Chapter Eleven

Ariadne didn't look up when she heard the bell chime on the shop door. She was halfway down an aisle in the back room, searching for a book title she'd been certain they had. Besides, she'd been disappointed too many times in the past few days. He wasn't coming after her. She should have figured that out by now.

"What were you doing outside, Ari?" Laurie asked. A short pause was followed by, "You're not Ari, are you?"

Almost stumbling in her haste, the real Ariadne abandoned her book search and hurried back into the main room of the shop. "No, I'm Fay," she heard her sister say. "And this is my grandmother, Lila Allandale."

Suddenly anxious, Ariadne glanced beyond the two of them, through the shop windows toward the parking lot. A single empty car was parked in the dooryard. No one else had come with them.

Fay understood both Ariadne's relief and her stinging disappointment. In a gentle voice, so low that the others couldn't hear, she confirmed her twin's conclusion. "Clay's still in Hartford."

As Laurie introduced herself and generously invited Ariadne's sister and grandmother to stay in her guest rooms, Ariadne chided herself once again for thinking Clay might come after her. When, she wondered, was she going to stop jumping every time the phone rang, thinking it might be him? At least she'd stopped running to see who'd come in every time the door opened.

A wry smile tugged at her lips. The old Ariadne had been sensible, but somewhere in the search for her identity she'd lost that trait, at least where Clay Franklin was concerned.

"I've left George," Lila announced.

"You mean to divorce him?" Ariadne was surprised to find that she was genuinely shocked by that notion.

"Of course not. That would be too easy on him." Lila's eyes twinkled, for a moment reminding Ariadne of Miss Emily. She'd have to see to it that the two women met while Lila was in Maine.

"Then…what?"

"That pigheaded old man needs some sense knocked into him and I finally realized that all I've been doing is… What's that word, Fay?"

"Enabling."

"Yes. Enabling. Almost the way wives of alcoholics keep buying the liquor for their husbands. I *agreed* with him. It was easier that way. More peaceful. Well, not anymore. Not about this. He actually thought we could take Shanna away from you! Until he comes to his senses, he'll have to make do with Rover for company."

Blinking at Lila, Ariadne tried to follow her logic. "Then you'll take him back?"

"Well, of course I will." She seemed surprised Ariadne would even ask. "But not until he admits he was wrong. Now, where's that adorable great-granddaughter of mine?"

"Shanna is at day care but it's almost time for her to come home." Ariadne glanced at her watch. "In fact, one of the other mothers should be dropping her off here at any minute."

"I'll hold the fort," Laurie offered. "Why don't you show Fay and Lila to the rooms they'll be sleeping in during their visit. You know which ones I use for guests."

By the time Ariadne had carried Lila's suitcase upstairs, Shanna had arrived. They could see the dooryard from the bedroom window. "I can't wait," the older woman exclaimed. She clattered back downstairs and off toward the shop, leaving Ariadne and Fay behind.

"Which room is mine?" Fay asked.

"In here." Ariadne opened the next door along the hall, the one Shanna sometimes used for naps, and both of them went in.

"He loves you, you know," Fay said as she hung a designer garment bag in the spacious closet. "He's just afraid to admit it."

A tiny ray of hope gleamed briefly, then faded away. "I don't think so, Fay. If he did, I'd have heard from him by now." She had to be practical. Forget Clay. Get on with her own life.

"He thinks you ran out on him."

"You've talked to him? He said that?"

Hypocrite, she thought. *What else was he to think? I did run away.*

"Not exactly." Fay toyed with the name tag on her matching flight bag. "I've only seen him once and that was mainly to talk about Gary and me. We're going to try a reconciliation."

"That's great." Ariadne had to force herself to sound encouraging and she had a feeling her twin was not all that happy about her situation, either. Fay was extracting a lacy camisole from the small bag, successfully hiding her expression in the process. "*Is* it great?" Ariadne asked.

"I guess I'll find out." The flash of a too-bright smile betrayed her uncertainty.

"When?"

"Whenever. In the meantime, I've taken a few more days of vacation so I can spend some time with you."

"Your logic is even harder to follow than your grandmother's," Ariadne complained. "Shouldn't you be spending the time with Gary? I mean, if you really want to work things out, it might be easier to be in the same state."

Dropping the burgundy-colored cashmere sweater she'd just lifted out of her bag, Fay turned to her sister and hugged her fiercely. "I'll do that after I've convinced you to do the same. You have to try for a reconciliation, too, Ari. At least talk to each other. I hate seeing a stupid misunderstanding ruin the lives of two people I love."

"You're exaggerating," Ariadne protested, disentangling herself.

"I don't think I am."

"Maybe it's better to let go." Ariadne thought that

might apply to Fay as well as herself. Her sister didn't seem very enthusiastic about starting over with Gary.

"You can't just give up," Fay insisted. "That's what our parents did. Nana was talking about them on the drive up here. She thinks they were star-crossed lovers, that they would have gotten back together again if other people hadn't interfered."

"That may be, but I'm not my mother and it isn't as if Clay and I have been married and split up. We're virtually strangers. And, frankly, I'm having trouble believing he cares what becomes of me. He finished the job he was asked to do and that was that. It's over."

Looking thoughtful, Fay paused in the act of shaking out a tightly rolled flannel nightgown perfect for the cold nights ahead. "I'm sure you know best." She essayed a theatrical sigh. "In time, I suppose you'll find someone else, marry, have more kids—"

Unable to stop herself, Ariadne protested. "No, I won't! I—"

The impish grin on her twin's face told Ariadne that she'd given her true feelings away. Well, what of it? She couldn't imagine replacing Clay. If the two of them had no future, then she'd just have to do without both lover and husband. She'd managed well enough before he came into her life.

"Don't you want more children?" Fay's wistful look said a good deal about her own desire to have a family.

"I've thought about it. But I have Shanna. Not every woman needs a husband and a houseful of kids in order to lead a fulfilling life. And my happiness certainly shouldn't have to depend on the constant presence of a man."

"Of course not," Fay agreed, "but wouldn't it be

nice if each woman could find the one man with whom she could share happiness? And children."

Certain now that her twin was thinking about her own situation, Ariadne reached out and touched Fay's forearm. "Is there... I mean, I can see how you took to Shanna. You'd make a wonderful mother."

Excited voices drifted up to them as Shanna and Lila began to climb the stairs in search of Mommy and Aunt Fay.

"There's no physical reason I can't have children. Gary just hasn't ever been enthusiastic about starting a family. I'm hoping I can change his mind."

Ariadne kept her thoughts to herself. It didn't work that way. Men didn't make radical changes in themselves just because they wanted to please a woman. Hoping one would was an exercise in futility. If anyone changed, it would be the woman. Ariadne grimaced as she realized she was a perfect example.

Shanna burst into the room, putting an end to any further discussion of Fay's marriage. "Mommy! Aunt Fay! Guess what I did today!"

Too bad grown-ups have to worry about the future, Ariadne thought. She envied her four-year-old's ability to live entirely in the present. And her boundless optimism.

Pessimism wasn't Ariadne's usual outlook, any more than cynicism was. She told herself she was just being realistic when she prepared herself for more trouble ahead. George Allandale was not the apologizing type, nor would he react well to being pressured into doing something he didn't want to do. Lila wasn't going to be able to change him any more than Fay was going to be able to change Gary. And if they could not succeed, then Ariadne found it difficult to believe there was a chance in the world that anything would ever change between herself and Clay.

Clay had been telling himself all week that Ari had deserted him, that he ought to forget all about her and get on with his career. The lectures did no good. He missed being with her. Worse, his life seemed appallingly empty. Meaningless. Futile. Knowing Ariadne Palmer had made him realize just how badly he needed to make some changes. If he kept going the way he was, he'd end up becoming like George Allandale— old, bitter, alone, and so fixated on control that he could no longer recognize any emotion softer than hatred.

"Clay? Got a minute?"

Barbara stood in the doorway. For the first time since she'd married his father, Clay took a long, hard look at her. Dressed for success in a man-tailored suit of bright magenta, her light brown hair cut shorter than Fay's, she appeared to be running on nervous energy. Makeup could not quite conceal the lines an edgy intensity had inscribed around her eyes and mouth. *Driven,* he decided, was the best word to describe her.

"What can I do for you, *Mom?*"

The reminder of their present relationship earned him a brittle smile as she entered his office and closed the door behind her to ensure privacy. A cloud of scent accompanied her. He didn't recognize it, but the perfume was perfect for Barbara, so strong it threatened to overwhelm anyone in her path.

Thoughts of Ari filled his mind. How could he have compared her to Barbara, even for a moment? Ari was nothing like this cold, calculating harpy.

"I'm divorcing your father," Barbara informed him.

Clay wasn't particularly surprised that their marriage

hadn't lasted. No wonder his father had been so upset the other day. But her blunt announcement did catch him off guard. "Why now?" he asked. "And why tell me?" If she thought she was rubbing salt in the wound of a broken heart, she'd seriously misread the reason he'd kept a careful distance between them during the past few years.

Arranging herself in a deceptively casual way in the client's chair, Barbara crossed one long, shapely leg over the other and flicked a bit of imaginary lint off the hem of her skirt. As a means of calling attention to her femininity, it couldn't be bettered.

"My partnership in the firm is sewn up nice and tight," she reminded him. "I'm in demand by our clients and as a result I no longer have the time to put up with the...demands of marriage. So I'm ready to divorce." She slid a calculating glance his way, then fixed her brightly colored lips in a patently false smile. "You're the best divorce lawyer in the business," she told him, then gave a little shrug, as if it galled her to make the admission.

If Clay hadn't already been seated, he'd have needed to find a chair. "Let me get this straight. You want me to represent you against my own father?"

"You *are* the best," she repeated.

"Conflict of interest, Barbara. You have heard of it, I presume?" He steepled his fingers, tipped back in his chair and affected boredom. She wasn't fooled.

"Conflict of interest wouldn't apply unless you were Clayton's lawyer, and I happen to know you aren't. There's no reason I can't hire you, as a consultant if nothing more."

Slowly he righted the chair, planting both feet firmly

on the carpet. He leaned across the desk and spoke each word clearly and distinctly. "No way in hell, Barbara."

"Don't you think you can be objective?" she taunted. "I'm sure you could talk yourself into it."

"What's that supposed to mean?"

Another shrug. "You're very good at talking yourself into believing that your client is the injured party. That's why you're so convincing in court. It's always so obvious that you're sure you're on the side of the angels."

Stung by the truth of her accusation, even though he'd recently come to the same conclusion himself, Clay made no reply. He *had* gotten good at lying to himself, an ironic situation indeed for someone who took such pride in never knowingly telling a lie to anyone else.

God, he was sick of divorces, disgusted by all the self-deception that went into obtaining one. Just to beat the odds, he hoped Fay and Gary could make their reconciliation work. Hell, he even hoped George could manage to convince Lila to come back to him.

"I don't suppose you and I would have lasted even this long," Barbara said. Her cool, speculative glance swept over him as she rose gracefully from her chair. "If you decide to represent your father, let me warn you right now that you won't find any loopholes in our prenuptial agreement."

"I don't intend to try."

Puzzled by his statement, she hesitated, one perfectly manicured hand on the doorknob. Clay pictured Ari's slim, firm hands. Her blunt-cut, unpolished nails were as natural and honest as she was.

Although Clay knew he couldn't affect the course of anyone else's relationship, he thought he might still have a chance to salvage his own. He saw it clearly now, a way to put an end to all the discontent in his life.

Partly to get a rise out of Barbara and partly to see how the concept sounded spoken aloud, Clay said, "I'm not taking on any more divorce cases."

Visibly shaken by this surprise announcement, and well aware of the effect it would have on the firm, Barbara momentarily lost her sophisticated facade and gaped at him. "But you're the best in the business. You command phenomenal fees."

Her astonishment was gratifying. Almost as gratifying as Clay's realization that his words had sounded damned good to him. He'd meant what he'd said.

Just that easily he made another decision. A weight he hadn't even been aware of shouldering, abruptly lifted.

"Think of the firm, Clay. Your father and the others if not me. You're a major draw for clients."

What had been only a small, self-satisfied smile widened into a grin. "I'm leaving the firm," he told her. "I'll be looking into the job situation in a much-smaller city."

Augusta, Maine, was the place he had in mind.

On the night before Fay was to return to Hartford, the two sisters sat together in her living room. With Shanna already tucked into bed and sound asleep and Lila on her way back to the guest room in Laurie's house, Fay once more demonstrated her ability to intuit things about her twin.

"You made love with him in Florida, didn't you?" she asked.

A furious blush answered her. Ariadne ducked her head, but it was too late to hide her reaction.

"I knew it. And that's why you mope around when you think no one's looking. You made a commitment to each other and you're miserable being apart."

"It was just sex, okay? It didn't mean anything." It shouldn't have, she told herself. It obviously hadn't to Clay.

"Of course it meant something. Do you think either one of you is the sort to hop into bed just to scratch an itch? Honestly, Ari! Dealing with Poppa is starting to look easy compared to making the two of you see what's right in front of your noses."

Try as she would, Ariadne couldn't quite keep a hopeful note out of her voice. "What do you mean?"

"I mean that you've inherited the Allandale stubborn streak and Clay ought to be related to us because he's being every bit as pigheaded about this as you are."

"The last thing he said to me was that we had unfinished business. I guess it's going to stay unfinished." Bitterness crept into her words. "Another lie."

"Clay never lies."

"He lied about our grandparents' situation. All that business about living at Hilltop Heights, buying the place furnished—"

"Well, they did. And I'll bet Clay never actually told you Poppa and Nana were poor. Did he?"

A flash of conversation came back to her. In the restaurant in Tarpon Springs. He'd said their real home was very different from the one she'd seen. She'd been the one who'd assumed that meant they were worse off than they appeared.

"I'll stake my life on it that he didn't." Fay placed one hand over her heart in an overly dramatic fashion but she was dead serious. "Clay doesn't say anything at all if he doesn't believe it's true."

"Then he's in the wrong business."

A nod signaled Fay's agreement with that observation. "You don't think he planned to become a divorce lawyer, do you? He just sort of fell into it. When he turned out to be good, he was pressured to keep taking more cases, for the sake of the law firm." Fay reached out and clasped her sister's hand. Her sad-eyed look spoke volumes. "Somewhere along the line, he started to believe that all marriages were doomed. I suppose that made it easier for him to convince himself that whatever his client told him was the truth. He's been wrong, Ari, but he doesn't lie. When he says something, he's absolutely certain that he's telling the whole truth and nothing but."

Remembering his conviction when they'd first met, his absolute assurance that she was who he said she was, Ariadne found she could accept Fay's claim. Unfortunately, that changed nothing.

"It doesn't matter what I feel, Fay. Okay. Yes. I love him. But it never would have worked. There was never anything more destined for us."

Unconvinced, Fay studied her twin's face. At last she sighed and threw up her hands in defeat. "All right. Have it your way. But now that we're a family, you and I and Shanna and Nana, at least, you'll have to accept that Clay will continue to play some role in your life. He's still my best friend, you know. For my sake, you're going to have to work out some kind of truce between you."

"I'll work on it," Ariadne promised. "Friendship."

When Fay left the apartment a short time later and Ariadne locked up after her, she wondered how on earth she'd ever keep that promise. Establish a platonic relationship with Clay? Think of him as Fay did, as a brother? Right now that didn't seem possible. Not as long as he was the man she knew she shouldn't love.

Clay reached Augusta at two o'clock in the morning. He rented a motel room, caught a few hours of sleep, had breakfast and then, timing matters so that he'd intercept Ari on her way back from taking Shanna to day care, set out to kidnap the woman he loved.

He pulled into the parking lot just as she was getting out of the station wagon. "Come for a short drive with me, Ari," he invited, reaching over to open the passenger side door of his dark green sedan. He gestured toward the bookstore. "We won't have any privacy in there with Laurie and Lila and Fay around."

Noting every nuance of her rapidly fluctuating expression, he took heart. She wasn't exactly flinging herself into his arms, but neither was she immune to him. In fact, if he wasn't mistaken, she was actually glad to see him. And annoyed. And unsure how to take his sudden reappearance.

"Fay left an hour ago," she said stiffly.

"And your grandmother?"

"Nana is still here. Miss Emily is spending the day with her. They've only just met, but they're getting on like a house afire."

"You're calling her Nana," Clay observed. "Progress." Lila had been in Maine less than a week. She worked fast.

Ari looked at him, then back at the shop. Framed in the display window, Laurie was making little shooing motions with her hands. "It's a conspiracy," Ari complained, but she got into the car.

Nervous at being alone with him, she clasped her hands in her lap and didn't say a word until she realized that he'd driven them straight to his motel.

"Clay, I don't think this is a good idea."

"We need privacy. To talk. This is private." He cut off further protest by getting out of the car and coming around to open her door for her. "I'm not planning to ravish you," he added, "just hold you prisoner for a while."

That she had to fight not to smile struck Clay as a good sign. He was even more encouraged when she got out of the car and followed him, unresisting, into his room, checking only briefly at the sight of the unmade bed.

"I thought about serenading you under your window in the wee hours of the morning, but I didn't think you'd appreciate the gesture." He hung the Do Not Disturb sign out and locked the door.

"How did things get so complicated?" she asked.

"Damned if I know. Can we start over, Ari? I have so much I want to tell you."

"Fay thinks you and I could become friends."

He hesitated, then took a step toward her, letting everything he felt for her show in his eyes. She drew in a sharp breath at what her frank perusal revealed and was unable to hide her response to it. He could read both love and longing in her gaze. Thank God. Without either one of them meaning to, they moved into each other's arms.

A gentle kiss feathered across Ariadne's brow.

For a moment longer she basked in the feeling of contentment, the afterglow of loving.

And then reality returned.

She was in Clay's bed, naked, sated…utterly appalled by her own behavior. "I must be losing my mind," she muttered.

"It will be all right, Ari. Trust me."

"I want to, but I'm not sure I should. You scramble my brains."

It was frightening how quickly she'd let go of common sense. There had been a powerful sexual pull between them right from the first and it was even stronger now that she knew how satisfying lovemaking was with him. She'd tumbled into that bed with barely a protest.

"Ari, I love you."

Pretending not to hear him, she flung herself out of the bed and began a frantic search for her discarded clothing. Everything was twisted and tangled. They'd been too frantic for each other to take much care in getting undressed.

"Come back to bed so we can talk this through." He rolled toward her but she stayed just out of reach.

"Talk? Right. We don't talk, Clay. We get too easily distracted. I knew this would happen. I should never have gotten into that car with you. I'm supposed to be at work right now. I don't have time to play games. I have responsibilities. I—"

Confronted by an uncompromisingly angry, intimidatingly naked man, she broke off. He seized her shoulders, bent his head and kissed her soundly. Her lips tingled by the time he stopped.

"We can dress if that makes you more comfortable but we have to talk, Ari. Didn't you hear me just now? I love you."

She closed her eyes against the sincerity that showed so plainly on his face. Love only complicated matters.

They had no future. Why did she keep forgetting that? He was a rich Connecticut divorce lawyer. Maybe they might end up being friends, for Fay's sake, but they were only torturing themselves to pretend that a romance could lead anywhere.

"You don't have to tell me you love me." She managed a false-sounding laugh. "This is just a brief, casual affair."

"Is it?"

"Of course. What else could it be? We're worlds apart."

A flicker of indecision crossed his face. His grip on her shoulders went slack, though he still didn't move his hands. "We need to talk," he said again. "It seems I have quite a few things to tell you."

Panic washed over her, bringing with it the fear that this man could tempt her to want to try to fit into his life. She reacted by grasping at straws. "Do you have something to tell me about George Allandale?"

With a sinking heart she felt his fingers tighten, saw his expression turn bleak. Fay was right. He didn't lie. She almost wished, just this once, that he would.

Letting go of her at last, he retrieved his rumpled clothes and started to dress. "One of the reasons I came to Augusta was to give Lila a message from her husband," he admitted.

"I should have known." She turned away from him and hastily finished putting on her clothing. He was working for Allandale.

Exasperation underlined his next words. "You don't have any faith in me at all, do you, Ari?"

"Why should I? You just said you came to see Nana. Obviously, all this—" she gestured blindly toward the bed "—was just an afterthought." What had been incredibly beautiful was suddenly unbelievably painful.

"You're deliberately misunderstanding." She heard the swish of denim as he pulled on his jeans, then the rasp of the zipper. "Do you take lessons in being difficult?"

Turning, she watched him button his shirt, waited for him to meet her eyes again, but when he did, she found she could read nothing there. He'd closed himself off from her.

Bitter disappointment lashed at her. Her voice was tight, her throat clogged with conflicting emotions, but she managed to choke out a few words, enough to let him know that Lila Allandale had a new ally and wasn't going to be browbeaten into going back to her husband.

Clay's expression was grim as he followed the sound of voices from Laurie's front door to the parlor. One belonged to Lila, the other to Miss Emily Vaughan. "Good afternoon, ladies," he greeted them as he stepped into the room.

"Why, Clay," Lila said, smiling. "What a pleasant surprise."

Anything but pleasantly surprised to see him, Miss Emily leveled a narrow-eyed look in his direction, one that put him in mind of an owl spotting a tasty mouse.

"Coffee?" Lila offered, gesturing toward the pot on the end table. "Of course, it is nearly time for lunch. You must stay and eat with us. Does Ariadne know you're here?"

"She's the one who told me where I'd find you. I have a message for you, Lila. From George."

Her needlework forgotten in her lap, she leaned forward in her chair. She made no effort to hide her eagerness for news.

"George has returned to Connecticut. He says, and I quote, 'I've come halfway. Now it's your turn.'"

Pursing her lips, Lila shook her head. "If that isn't just like him! He's sulking, you know."

"That may be, but I don't think he's prepared to compromise any further." Personally, Clay thought George Allandale was behaving like a jackass.

"There is an excellent firm of attorneys here in Augusta," Miss Emily remarked. "McClymer, Dorr and Gerritsen. I understand they're quite clever at property settlements."

"Hush, Emily."

"You ought to stay right here until George comes to his senses."

"There's only one problem," Lila told her new friend gently. "I love George, in spite of all his faults. And I fully intend to go back to him, now that he's admitted, after his own fashion, that he needs me."

A stunning smile on her face, Lila put down her coffee cup and rose with the grace of a queen. "Emily, dear, you'll have to excuse me. I need to go pack."

Although she looked as if she'd just tasted something sour, Miss Emily wished Lila well. "Have a safe flight," she added.

"I do wish I didn't have to fly back," Lila murmured, looking back hopefully at Clay as she headed toward the stairs. "I do so dislike those bumpy little planes."

"Sorry, Lila. I won't be driving back to Connecticut for some time."

An enigmatic expression on her face, Lila drifted away.

"Well, skunk-hunter?" Miss Emily demanded as soon as they were alone. "Exactly what are your intentions?"

Delighted by her old-fashioned turn of phrase, Clay found it easy to ignore the asperity in her tone. "I plan to ask Ariadne Palmer to marry me."

"She won't want to move out of state," Miss Emily warned.

"I know that. I don't intend to ask her to." Clay dropped down onto the sofa, thinking that she might be getting a crick in her neck looking up at him.

A skeptical frown put more crinkles in the old woman's round face. She was dressed all in blue today, Clay noticed, a definite improvement over prom pink.

"Commuter marriages rarely work," she informed him. "Best you move here."

"I've already decided to do just that. I'll be taking the Maine bar exam in a few months." A wry note entered his voice. "I'll need that long to review everything I learned in law school. This state has tougher requirements than most."

"And just when did you plan to tell all this to Ari?"

"Just as soon as I can get her alone again."

"She might say no. She's been a bit prickly lately."

"Don't worry, Miss Emily. I won't give up until she agrees. You see, I'll still love her if she turns me down. Hell, I even love her when she turns me inside out."

Very slowly, Miss Emily unbent. An almost-friendly gleam replaced her earlier, beady-eyed hostility. "You'll do," she said. "Now get off your duff and go pop the question." She used her *Boston Post* cane to point to the exit.

"Yes, ma'am," he said, and went.

"Well, well," Laurie greeted him when he entered the bookstore. "About time you showed up."

He held both hands out in front of him as he approached the counter. "Truce. I come in peace."

"You've got a lot to answer for, mister."

"Now, Laurie—"

She cut him off with an impatient gesture. "Ari said to tell you she'll be right back. She had to go pick up Shanna."

"Now?" He glanced at his watch, suddenly uneasy. "Isn't it pretty early for day care to let out?"

"The kid's sick."

Instant panic ripped through him. "How bad is it?"

Clay realized he was overreacting, but he couldn't help it, and if the idea of that little girl being sick shook him this much, he could only imagine how Ari must feel.

A gleam of amusement flickered behind Laurie's big, round glasses. "Don't get all riled up. I'm sure it's just some bug that's going around. She'll be fine as soon as she's tucked into bed with Mommy fussing over her."

An unwelcome realization dawned. If Shanna needed a lot of attention, that was going to complicate matters for him. He couldn't blame the little girl for being sick, but if Ari was worried and upset when she got back she wouldn't be in any mood to be wooed.

So much for all his romantic plans. He assumed he'd still be able to talk to Ari, though, to explain a few things, to tell her about the career changes he was going to make. But when Ari returned with Shanna, that alternative, too, had to be scrapped.

Shanna had the chicken pox.

In short order, Clay, who'd never had it, was not

only banned from Ari's apartment but told in no uncertain terms to go home.

"Oh, my dear boy!" Lila sympathized when she heard. "What terrible timing." She blinked and beamed at him. "On the other hand, there's no reason now why you can't offer me a ride back to Hartford."

"Might as well," Miss Emily told him. "None of us will do them any good by hanging around. Just get in the way. Besides, even though chicken pox is no big deal for a child, it can be downright dangerous for an adult."

Elaborating on her theme, she seemed to enjoy sharing every grisly detail she could dredge up out of personal experience and hearsay. A chat with Shanna's pediatrician confirmed enough of it to convince Clay that he was outvoted.

In the end, on the condition that he talk to Ari before he left, Clay reluctantly agreed to return to Connecticut until Shanna recovered. There were things he could do, but he hated having to leave so much unsettled. The meeting was hastily arranged. Conditions were not optimal.

Poised for flight on the small balcony outside her apartment, Ari frowned down at him as he started up the steps. "I have to get back to Shanna."

"Give me five minutes?"

"That should be more than enough. I already know you're working for my grandfather again."

"No, I'm not. In fact, I've never worked for George."

"You brought a message from him. Nana's going back with you."

"Only because I was coming here anyway. And her strategy worked. I haven't talked to George in person, but my father tells me he's desperate to get Lila back. He can barely function without her."

Skepticism made an effective barrier between them. Discouraged, Clay reassessed his decision to fill her in on his plans before he left. She had enough on her plate with Shanna sick. And it appeared she was still working through some pretty powerful feelings about her grandfather.

"He may surprise us all," Clay said. "He doesn't want to lose Lila." Cautiously he climbed another two steps, stopping only when she backed closer to her door.

"I doubt an old dog like him can learn any new tricks. Why should he try? Even Fay will probably forgive him."

"What about you, Ari? Can you forgive him?"

Can you forgive me?

Ari was quiet, staring at her hands, which were clasped in front of her. He wanted to reach out to her, to fold her fingers in his own, to reassure her. Waiting for some signal from her was harder than he'd ever imagined it could be. He prayed his patience would pay off.

"I'm glad to have been reunited with Fay and Nana, in spite of all the emotional upheaval that was involved. Their presence has enriched my life. and Shanna's." Suddenly aware that her choice of words might be taken wrong, she clarified that. "Enriched in ways that have nothing to do with money."

"I know." It had been difficult all along for him to be cynical about her. Now he admired her more than he could say. It took a strong woman to focus on the positive things that had come out of her wrenching discovery of not one, but two sets of family lies.

"As for George Allandale," Ari said, "I suppose I may eventually find it in my heart to forgive him, if he really does change." A muffled sound from inside the apartment distracted her. "I have to go in. Shanna needs me."

So much had to be left unsaid. There was no time left. And Ari, Clay sensed, was in no frame of mind to listen. Her focus, as it should be, was on the sick child waiting for Mommy to come back.

"Tell Shanna I'll see her soon."

Lips tight, eyes wary, she didn't need to say aloud that she thought he'd disappoint her daughter, disappoint her. "There's no reason for you to come visit again, Clay."

"No reason? What about the fact that we can't keep our hands off each other? What about—"

"That's just sex." Flustered by her own words and his challenging glare, her eyes slid away from his. She retreated as he climbed higher. He was more than halfway to her balcony when he halted his advance.

"We have a lot left to discuss," he reminded her, "but this isn't the time or place." She did have to get back to her daughter.

She might not be ready to admit how she felt, but he no longer had any doubts. Abruptly, he moved to close the distance between them, taking the last few steps two at a time. Her eyes widened and he was certain she thought he was going to haul her into his arms and kiss her. That was reason enough not to. Instead he took her left hand in both of his and pressed it, briefly, over his heart. He let his eyes speak for him. And then, when he knew she was as off balance as she would ever be, he let her go.

"I'll phone you," he called over his shoulder as he descended the stairs. "And I *will* be back."

Chapter Twelve

Clay surprised Ariadne by keeping his promise and calling her every evening during the next week. He wanted to come back to Maine for the weekend but she convinced him that he should stay away a few more days, just to be on the safe side.

It was not infection she was worried about.

It was her heart.

He was a walking temptation to her, and only when they were apart could she manage to convince herself that simple friendship was an admirable goal. It might even be attainable...as long as they didn't get within touching distance.

By Monday morning, ten days after Shanna had come down with the chicken pox, the little girl was well enough to go back to day care, but Ariadne was exhausted. The long hours of nursing had taken their toll.

Laurie wanted her to stay home and sleep, but she returned to work anyway. She answered the phone when it rang, an hour after opening, without feeling the slightest premonition of disaster.

Five minutes later, fighting a sense of panic that threatened to overwhelm her, she hung up. Her hands were shaking when she turned toward Laurie. They were the only ones in the bookstore, though Ariadne wouldn't have noticed if an entire brass band had been present.

"What? Who was on the phone? Has Shanna had a relapse?"

Shaking her head, incapable for a moment of putting what she was thinking into words, Ariadne gripped the edge of the counter with both hands for support. She felt as if she'd been bushwhacked. Her knees were actually wobbly.

"That was your dear cousin, Brad."

If she'd been thinking clearly she'd have asked him how he'd even heard that Shanna had been stricken with the chicken pox. Then again, she probably wouldn't have been able to get a word in edgewise, what with all his accusations about how she was an unfit mother. Apparently there was now a vaccine for chicken pox and he claimed she had neglected her child by failing to have Shanna inoculated.

Barely aware that Laurie was shooting questions at her, offering help, whatever the problem was, Ariadne stared at the telephone. Maybe her common sense still wasn't functional, what with this threat coming on top of being so worn-out, but her fingers didn't hesitate as they tapped out the number of Clay's apartment in Hartford. When no one answered, she tried the car phone.

It was already ringing when her brain belatedly kicked in. He'd be at his office by this hour. She was about to disconnect when he picked up.

"I need your advice," she blurted.

"Ari? What's wrong?"

Overwhelmed both by the depth of her need to share her burden with Clay and the relief she felt in knowing he was there for her, Ariadne had to swallow hard before she could answer. She was on the verge of tears but refused to give in to them. "It's Shanna's father," she told Clay. "He's threatening to sue me for her custody."

Clay heard the note of suppressed hysteria in her voice, though, without breaking down, she managed to repeat everything Brad had said to her. The man was scum, and his threats nothing less than psychological abuse. Clay was careful to keep his own tone as calm and reassuring as possible, no small feat given the intense anger he felt. Brad Comfort ought to be taken out and shot.

"That business about the vaccination is nothing to worry about," he told Ari, "and I'd be very surprised if he ever got a case that shaky to court." He'd had Duncan do a little investigating. Comfort didn't have the financial resources to be more than a nuisance.

"Why does he want Shanna? Why now? It doesn't make any sense."

"At a guess, he's getting pressure from his wife."

Silence. Clay wished he could see Ari's face, that he could guess what she was thinking. How much should he tell her? Clay didn't believe Celia Comfort posed any real threat. Duncan considered her as the flighty type, always jumping from one enthusiasm to another. In all likelihood, all Ari would have to do was wait them out. Mentioning Duncan, though, would stir up old conflicts. He was reluctant to bring up the private investigator's name.

"Ari? You've got nothing to worry about. Trust me. No one's going to take Shanna away from you."

"I overreacted, didn't I?" She sounded subdued, almost too calm. Embarrassed? Maybe.

"A little," he said carefully, "but panic is perfectly understandable. I'm glad you called me."

Clay stared through the car's windshield at the quiet street in front of his condominium. Ari probably thought she'd caught him on his way to the office. In reality he would have been on the road, en route to Maine, in another half hour or so. He was about to tell her that he'd be there by midafternoon when an uncomfortable thought struck him. Had she reached out to the man? Or to the lawyer with a reputation for winning divorce and custody cases?

"Is there any way to convince Brad to drop the whole idea? I hate the thought of this dragging on and on." She was asking the lawyer, Clay concluded. But maybe, just maybe, she'd also known instinctively that she could count on him as a friend. He decided to regard that as progress.

"Let me check into a couple of possibilities and get back to you," he said. After a few more words of reassurance he broke the connection.

For a short time longer he sat in his car, wondering if he'd made another mistake with Ari. Ten nights in a row he'd avoided telling her about his plans. He'd had ample opportunity during those lengthy telephone conversations to confess that he was moving to Maine, to tell her that he loved her and wanted to marry her. Instead, he'd talked about the past, in particular his childhood. He'd learned more about her life. They'd found at least a hundred likes and dislikes they had in common. In fact, they'd discussed just about everything under the sun except their future. She didn't know how powerfully she affected him. Neither did she suspect anything about his intention to move to Maine. She had no idea that he'd quit his job. He hadn't wanted to explain all that over the phone. He wanted to be face-to-face with Ari when he told her.

Had the carefully platonic tone of those conversations been the mistake? Or was it what had happened in that motel room in Maine? He did regret giving her the impression that he was only interested in sex. She was probably convinced he didn't know the difference between love and lust.

Aware that indecision wasn't getting him anywhere, Clay got out of the car and headed inside. It was too late for regrets now. He told himself he wasn't really all that pessimistic about how she'd react. After all, she'd called him, even if it was only in a crisis. Even with so much unsettled between them, she'd known she could count on him. They'd sort this out, in person.

He knew how to plead a case and win.

Boxes overflowing with books and papers and furniture covered with dust sheets filled his once-pristine living room. It had never looked more lived-in than it did now that he was moving out. The last of the suitcases he'd packed for an indefinite stay was waiting in the bedroom. The apartment was ready to close up. The Realtor would list it as of the first of next week.

Self-confidence increased as he scanned the familiar surroundings. There was nothing he would miss about this place, this life. He knew what he wanted now.

Absence definitely did make the heart grow fonder.

If nothing else, their long-distance courtship had let them get to know each other without being distracted by the intense chemistry between them. Proof, he believed, that what he'd suspected all along was true. There was much more than lust between them. There was love. They had a future. All he had to do was convince Ari of that.

As he started the engine and pulled away from the sterile complex that had been his home for the last five years, in his mind Clay replayed what Ari had said. A new, irritatingly possible explanation occurred to him. He wasn't being cynical, he decided. If his suspicions were correct, one brief stop on the way north would clear things up.

By the time he drove to the Allandales' Connecticut estate, Clay's hunch had solidified into a certainty. He didn't like what he was thinking, but it made a perverted kind of sense.

George was in his study, a room eerily similar to the office in his Tarpon Springs house. "I'm getting tired of playing this scene, George," Clay told him when he stalked in. "No one, I repeat, no one, is going to take Shanna away from her mother."

"Why aren't you in Maine?" George demanded, not bothering to deny the accusation. "You're supposed to be in Augusta, rescuing my granddaughter."

"Since when did she become acceptable, George? Or is this some convoluted scheme to get you custody of that little girl?"

He looked hurt. All an act? Clay wasn't sure of anything with George anymore. "Everything I do is in Ariadne's best interests."

"That's why you suggested to Brad Comfort that he sue her for custody of Shanna?"

"I created a situation in which Ariadne would turn to you for help and me for money. You gave me the idea yourself, telling me you'd thought Comfort might want the child." George sounded insufferably pleased with his own cleverness.

"Doesn't it occur to you that you've taken a risk, encouraging a man like Comfort?"

"I can always pay him off."

"What if his wife really wants Shanna? What if they win custody?"

"You're too good a lawyer."

"Not in Maine. It'll be months yet before I can even take the bar exam, and it's one of the toughest around. I might not pass the first time."

George waved that aside, as usual ignoring anything he didn't want to hear. "I can hire the best available in Maine, then. The point is, she needs our help. I just hope she also has sense enough to marry you."

"I'd appreciate being allowed to do my own courting." Exasperation had his jaw clenched and his muscles taut. Much more of George's kind of help and Clay figured he'd be lucky if Ari ever spoke to him again.

"Get her to say yes by the end of the month and I'll pay for the wedding."

"I'd sooner elope!" Why was he wasting his time? Better to head north, to Ari. He'd concentrate on convincing her that he loved her. It was going to take some effort. Thanks to George, she had little reason to believe anyone associated with the Allandales.

"Surely you wouldn't deprive her grandmother and me of a big wedding?" George had a "poor-me" look on his face, but Clay didn't fall for it. This was just one more trick to manipulate all of them. He wanted grandchildren and had decided this was the way to get them.

"Get this straight, George. How Ari and I feel toward each other and what we do about it has nothing to do with you. If we do marry, it won't be for your sake, or at your convenience."

The sound of applause startled them both. From the look of dawning dismay on his face, George had forgotten anyone else was in the room.

The high back of a Queen Anne chair pulled close to a picture window hid Lila from view until she stood, her embroidery still in her hands. She'd been there all along, listening and waiting for the right moment to intervene. Now she turned on her husband, pointing a vicious-looking, curved needle at him for emphasis as she advanced.

"Now, Lila—"

"Don't you 'now Lila' me you pigheaded moron. Do you have any idea what you've done? When Ariadne finds out about this latest trick, she'll give up on you completely."

Clay had a fleeting impression of stalker and prey that would have amused him if he hadn't been so irritated by the entire situation.

"No need to tell her my part in it," George said hastily.

"There's every need," Clay disagreed. "There have been enough lies." There would be no more. Ever.

Very carefully Lila set her needlework on the desk. George watched her with wary eyes.

"Let me put this in simple terms for you, George. You drove Phyllis away by trying to run her life for her. You've come close to doing the same thing with Fay more times than I can count. There might have been a reason for Fay and Ariadne to give you a second chance if you hadn't gone and meddled again, but now you've ruined everything. You've done this to yourself, George. It's your own fault that you'll never see Shanna again.''

Coldly analytical, utterly without compassion for the man she'd been married to for so many years, Lila ignored the anguished look in George's eyes. She lashed out again, reminding him of the physical resemblance between Shanna and Phyllis, bringing home to him that, through his own actions, he'd destroyed any hope of getting his daughter back in the person of her granddaughter.

"You've been hateful," Lila told him. "Manipulative and judgmental. And you just keep repeating the same mistakes.''

Slowly dawning horror twisted George's features as he saw himself clearly for the first time. Suffering under the weight of that devastating self-knowledge, he backed away, but there was no escape.

"You're going to be alone, George," Lila threatened. "Unless you do something to redeem yourself, and make a real effort to change, you're going to lose all of us.''

A long, pregnant pause ensued before he swallowed hard and asked, "How?" The look of desperation in his eyes was enough to convince Clay that this, at least, was no act.

It wouldn't be easy on either of them, Clay thought as he quietly left the room, but he had a feeling that Lila would prevail. George would be forced to face up to all his shortcomings. He might even manage to overcome a few of them.

* * *

"I'm having second thoughts about calling Clay," Ariadne told Laurie. "What can he do from Connecticut? And what if he misinterprets my reasons for contacting him? What if he thinks I want him to rush back here?"

"You mean, what if he reads them correctly? Admit it, Ari. You miss him."

Had she used the threat to Shanna as an excuse? That was an awful thing to have done...if she had. Ariadne hated feeling this confused, this helpless.

She'd behaved like some brainless bimbo who couldn't handle her own problems. She wanted to see Clay again. Yes. That was true enough. And he had promised to come back, and now that Shanna was over the chicken pox, he could. But in all those phone conversations over the past ten days, he'd never once repeated his declaration of love. As far as Ariadne knew, he might have decided he wanted no more from her than the same sort of friendship he had with Fay.

"I'm not helpless," she said aloud. And she was well past the overreacting stage. She was still tired, but at least her brain was fully functional once more.

Brad hadn't even met Shanna yet. Neither had his new wife. "I should be shot for what I'm thinking," Ariadne muttered. "Mothers are supposed to insist their children are little angels."

"What are you babbling about now?" Laurie demanded.

"There may be an easy way to put an end to Brad's threats. What if I invite his new wife over here to meet Shanna? Say this afternoon when she gets home from her first day back at day care? From what you've told me, the woman has no experience with kids, let alone four-year-olds. And Shanna's likely to be cranky.''

"An hour ought to do it," Laurie agreed with a grin.

"Are you calling my daughter a brat?"

"Nope. Just a normal child. Celia won't know what hit her.''

Celia.

Saying her name aloud made her much too real. And reality carried with it an element of risk. "What if she adores Shanna? I mean, I can't count on my daughter being overtired and irritable when she gets home from day care.''

"Give yourself some backup, then," Laurie suggested, pushing the phone across the counter. "Call Mrs. Pritchard and see if her kid—what's her name? Mary Anne? Mary Jo?''

"Mary Sue."

"Right. See if dear little Mary Sue can come here to play this afternoon. I guarantee that between the two of them they'll put Celia off motherhood for life.''

After hours of driving, made to seem longer by a steady, early-April downpour, Clay reached Augusta. He considered going directly to Ari's bookstore, but decided to make one short stop first. He wanted everything settled before he saw her again.

It was just after four in the afternoon when he was shown into the inner office of Comfort Real Estate. "Nice place you've got here," he said with a cursory glance at his surroundings. To judge by the leather upholstery and the original artwork on the walls, business had been good before the recent slump. Duncan's report had indicated that for the past six months, ever since Comfort's wedding, in fact, business finances had been touch and go.

"What do you want, Franklin?"

"I'd think that was obvious. I'm here to tell you that Shanna is not a pawn you can use to make deals with the Allandale Company."

"Allandale already phoned." Comfort's surliness told Clay volumes about that conversation.

Apparently George's redemption had already begun. Score one for Lila. Clay had no sympathy for Brad Comfort. He'd gotten something out of the old man, just not as much as he'd hoped for.

"I'm speaking for myself," Clay warned him. "Leave Ariadne and Shanna alone from now on. They're no longer your concern."

"That kid is my flesh and blood. I've got rights."

Contemptuously Clay informed him he'd given up any rights he might have had a long time ago.

"Who'd have thought little Ariadne Palmer would turn out to have a stinking rich granddaddy," he muttered. "I'd have married her if I'd known that."

"You'd have been divorced by now."

He wasn't being cynical. He had learned to have faith in Ari's good judgment. She might have married him, for Shanna's sake, but she'd have had the good sense to send him packing the minute she discovered what he was really like.

"Your loss, Comfort," he commiserated. "You're out of the loop now. If you want a child, you'll have to talk to your own wife."

"Fat chance," said a strident female voice.

"Mrs. Comfort, I presume." Clay turned slowly. She was an attractive blonde but her looks were marred by the petulant expression on her face.

Ready to leave anyway, his message delivered, Clay retreated to the outer office, but Celia Comfort had a carrying voice and Clay had to take the time to slip into his raincoat, didn't he?

"I've just met your daughter, Bradley," she announced.

Shamelessly eavesdropping now, Clay smiled at the hint of temper he heard in her voice.

"I thought you'd lost interest in her?" Comfort retorted. "You only mentioned her that one time and then you got ticked off at me when I did what I thought you wanted and went and talked to her mother."

"I was curious, just as I was curious when I first found out she existed. I don't like secrets, Bradley."

"And I don't like that tone of voice. Just spit it out, Celia. What's got you in a lather this time?"

"I want to know how Ms. Palmer got the idea I wanted to raise her child."

"How would I know?"

"There were two of them, Bradley." Clay could almost hear the shudder in her voice. "They kept singing this little tune, over and over again. 'Happy happy, joy joy!' until I thought I would go mad."

"Celia, I never—"

"No, *I* never, Bradley. Children are far more trouble than they're worth. You and I will not be having any."

When Clay left his listening post he almost felt sorry for Brad Comfort. The man had missed his chance to have a loving wife and daughter. He'd never know the happy happy joy joy Clay hoped to share with them.

The drive across the city, however, gave him just enough time to start to worry. What if he was wrong? What if Ari didn't love him? What if this last bit of meddling on George's part proved to be too much for her? She was already having trouble believing in him because of all the lies other people had told her. Even if she did love him, he could still blow it. Especially when she learned he'd been keeping more secrets from her. He'd made elaborate plans for the future without even consulting her.

Clay knew his only option was to confess everything, not just what he'd found out about the reason behind Brad's threat but what he'd been up to himself. From the sound of it, Ari had dealt quite handily with Brad and Celia without his help. All he could do was assure her she'd succeeded in discouraging Mrs. Comfort. She no longer had to worry about anyone trying to take Shanna away from her.

On his way into the bookstore, Clay flipped the Closed sign over and locked the door behind him. He stopped just inside to stare at the slender, dark-haired woman seated on a high stool behind the antique cash register. He couldn't help himself. Even though he'd tried to prepare for this meeting, the fact of actually being here in her presence again unnerved him.

What bothered him even more was the jolt of sexual awareness he felt. The whisper of her skirt against the silk slip beneath had desire slamming into him. All she had to do was look up from her paperwork and suddenly he was drowning in the biggest brown eyes he'd ever seen.

"Clay," Ariadne said, her voice faintly husky and altogether appealing.

As she slid off the stool and came around the counter toward him, a whiff of perfume preceded her, just a faint, sweet fragrance, but enough to trigger a brief vision of a field full of wildflowers and Ariadne in a gauzy dress.

When she moved near enough to touch, Clay's carefully thought out plans went right out the window. He hadn't planned the kiss that consumed them both. He'd intended to keep his distance, to speak his piece and let her decide, rationally, what she wanted to do.

One touch of her lips to his and he wasn't himself anymore. Or maybe he was more himself than he'd ever been.

It didn't matter. He couldn't resist her. As the kiss deepened, he admitted that he'd been lost since the first time he'd come into this shop and seen her. Everything that had happened between them had been inevitable. The only thing that was still in doubt was their happy ending.

Ariadne couldn't control her helpless response to him. She'd been as full of tension as an overwound clock all day, poised to strike or stop dead at any moment. Clay's arrival unleashed all that tightly wound energy. She gave herself over to the sheer rapture of being in his arms again.

"I can't seem to stop wanting you," Clay whispered. "And it's so much more than a sexual yearning. I miss your wit, your humor, your warmth. I even miss your daughter."

The mention of Shanna brought Ariadne back to her senses with a jolt. How could she admit to Clay that she'd gotten him here on false pretenses?

"About Shanna," she began.

He didn't let her finish. "Relax, Ari. There isn't a chance in hell that Brad and his new wife will ever take your daughter away from you."

"I wasted your time, making you drive all the way up here. I'm sorry. I overreacted."

"I was coming back anyway. And I'm glad you called me when you needed help."

"I haven't been acting like myself at all today." She wanted to tell him what else she'd done, but before she could he touched his finger to her lips to quiet her and launched into a confession of his own.

She listened, astonished and yet not really surprised, to an account of her grandfather's latest machinations. The manipulative old meddler had offered Brad a bribe to make his threat. And she was supposed to have done...exactly what she had done. Call Clay.

"Well, that explains it," she said.

"Explains what?" he asked as she ducked behind the counter and came up with a large scrapbook.

"This. It came by special messenger about twenty minutes ago. From my grandfather. It's an album he apparently kept of my mother's work, her photographs when they were published in a magazine she once worked for. It looks as if he was proud of her, Clay, even if he was too stubborn to tell her so. That he kept the album all this time must mean something."

"But why send it to you? Was there a note?"

There was. It said simply "I was wrong. Can we start again?" and was signed "Poppa." Ariadne had to smile at the look of amazement on Clay's face when he read that.

"Now that you've filled in some details, this peace offering makes more sense. It sounds like Nana has him well in hand." She cautioned herself not to expect too much. In her experience, men were resistant to change. Women were the ones who were expected to be accommodating...if they wanted a relationship. The other option was to do without, to admit that it was impossible to have it all.

She sighed deeply.

"It's up to you to decide if you can forgive him."

Ariadne had a feeling Clay wasn't just talking about George Allandale. She thought she understood what he was really saying, that she understood him, but she wasn't quite ready to test her conclusions yet. It felt safer to keep talking about her grandfather.

"He *is* family," she said. "They do say you can choose your friends, but family..."

"So you think you'll work things out? Let him see Shanna now and again?"

"I'm willing to think about it."

He nodded, seeming pleased. "Are we alone?" he asked. "No customers hiding in the stacks?"

"Yes. Laurie's gone to preview an auction. I just have to lock up."

"Already done." He guided her toward one of the comfortable reading nooks, one with a love seat, one that was out of sight of the windows. "Where's Shanna?"

"Mary Sue's mother invited her to have supper with them, since I had both girls earlier this afternoon."

"So we can talk?"

Ariadne blushed. "Only if you *mean* to talk this time. No...distractions."

And yet, sitting this close to him, the last thing Ariadne really wanted was conversation. She had to give herself a stern lecture about the dangers of giving in to passion, about the necessity of protecting herself from future heartbreak. She had to think of Shanna's well-being.

And she had to look out for Clay's happiness, too.

What she kept dreaming about for all three of them was surely impossible. She couldn't ask it of him.

They'd talked before about how some change was inevitable, and that it was often good, but she loved him too much to demand that he change completely. His life was in Hartford. He'd made a name for himself there in his field. He would never offer to give all that up, and if she asked it of him and he tried and failed, then all his cynical predictions about love and marriage would come true.

She had to be strong. For all their sakes.

"You said a few minutes ago that you choose your friends, but not your family. That's not quite true, Ari. You do choose one part of your family."

"Not very well sometimes." She didn't pretend to misunderstand him. What would be the point? "Once upon a time, I thought I wanted to marry Brad."

"I've been wrong in the past, too. I'll tell you all about it sometime. The thing you have to know now, though, is that I think you were absolutely brilliant."

"What?" Genuinely confused, she just stared at him. This was not the next turn their "talk" was supposed to take.

"I stopped at Brad's office on my way here. While I was there, his wife returned from her visit with Shanna."

Heat rose into her face. "Oh" was all she could manage to say. So he knew. She supposed she'd hoped to leave him with a good impression of her. It saddened her to learn that he now knew the worst about her.

"Your plan worked. If she never spends time with another four-year-old it will be too soon."

"Oh."

"Oh? Is that all you can say? I'd think you'd be ecstatic."

"Why? Because I've obviously inherited some of

George Allandale's talent for manipulating people?'' Ariadne fought off a wave of emotion and added brokenly, ''I'm so ashamed of myself, Clay. I used my own child to deceive that woman. I—''

He made a sound that might have been a laugh and seized her shoulders, giving her a shake until she was forced to look at him again. There was no censure in his gaze. ''You did what you had to do to protect yourself,'' Clay said firmly. ''And Shanna.''

''But it wasn't even necessary,'' she wailed.

''It might have been. George contacted Brad, not Celia.''

Panic lanced through Ariadne, wiping out her bout of remorse. ''You think she might change her mind?'' Even though she knew she was overreacting again, she could not seem to stem the tide of irrational, frightening thoughts. ''When Shanna is older she won't be such a handful. Celia might—''

That Clay suddenly looked uncertain worried Ariadne even more. She broke off and just stared at him, willing him to say something to relieve her fears.

Slowly he dropped his hands from her shoulders. She missed the contact and had to clasp her own hands tightly in her lap to keep from reaching for him.

''Clay, you're scaring me.''

''You're the best mother in the world,'' Clay assured her.

''Then what are you thinking? Why do you look so...troubled.''

''You want to know what I'm thinking? Exactly what I'm thinking, no matter how...inappropriate it is?''

Perplexed by his strange choice of words, she nodded.

"I warn you, this may make me seem as manipulative as George Allandale."

"I can hardly criticize anyone on that score. Not after what I did to Celia." Impatient now, Ariadne grabbed his arm. "Tell me."

"You won't think less of me?"

"Are you trying to make me lose my temper?"

He looked thoughtful. "I may be. You're beautiful when you're angry, Ari."

She smacked him, just the way she'd seen Fay smack him, and he laughed. Then, abruptly serious again, he put his hand over hers where it still gripped his forearm.

"Okay. No lies between us. I was thinking that there'd be one sure way to make certain Brad never tried to take you to court over a custody issue. All you have to do is provide the one thing he can claim Shanna lacks."

Her heart began to beat a little faster. "What's that?"

"A two-parent family. You and me, Ari."

"Are you suggesting that I marry you to protect Shanna?"

His sheepish smile charmed her even as his words made her confusion greater. "Makes sense to me."

She put a little distance between them, struggling to keep things light. Maybe she was reading too much into this. Maybe she didn't understand him, after all.

"I know you like my daughter, but you don't need to go to such extremes just for Shanna's sake."

"How about for *my* sake? You see, I've done several very selfish things this last week." He ticked them off on his fingers, but his eyes never left her face. He was looking for her approval. That realization stunned her into silence.

"I resigned from the law firm. I put my condo on the market. I made arrangements to take the bar exam here in Maine."

Swallowing hard, Ariadne could only manage to choke out a single word. "Why?"

"I'm moving to Augusta."

"Why?" This time her voice was a little steadier, but she felt just as nervous.

"A number of reasons. For one thing, the time I spent here with you last month made me take a long hard look at what I'd become. I didn't like what I saw. I didn't like where I was heading. Fortunately, I'm still young enough to start over." He grinned at her and she smiled weakly back. "When I set up my new law practice here, I won't be handling any divorces. You see, I've come to realize that there may be something to this marriage business after all. With the right person."

Sitting very still, scarcely daring to breathe, Ariadne struggled for calm reason. She couldn't let herself get her hopes up. Not yet. So far, he'd only said what a friend might say.

And they had become friends this past week, during those long-distance phone calls. Yet never once in any discussion had he mentioned the radical changes he was making in his life.

"What if you realize...a month from now...a year from now, that you were wrong? What if you miss your old life? Your old friends?" *Your old lovers?*

"I won't. Of course, there is one other change I've been contemplating, one that would make my new life utterly fulfilled and complete. I want you to be part of it, Ari.''

As a friend? She was steeling herself to ask that question aloud when he stunned her by sliding off the love seat and going down on one knee in front of her. He took her hand in his and lifted it to his lips, kissing first the back, then the palm. When he looked up at her again, his heart was in his eyes.

''Will you marry me, Ariadne Palmer? I love you so much that I can no longer imagine the rest of my life without you in it.''

Still she hesitated. ''How can you be so sure? All these changes...and I've changed, too, in just the short time you've known me. I'm having a regular identity crisis.'' She tried to laugh and failed. ''What if I'm still changing? What if I turn into my grandfather?''

''Which one?''

''*Either* one.''

''Then I will be very surprised. You are yourself first, Ari, and that person is the one I love. We'll grow and change together. That is, if you'll have me. If you can find it in your heart to love me.''

I never stopped loving you. She opened her mouth to say the words aloud, but Clay wasn't done yet.

''I know that first you'll have to come to trust me again. Can you do that much, Ari? Will you believe me when I tell you that I love you and that I want to marry you?''

A joyousness she'd never before experienced filled her heart. ''You've never lied to me, Clay. I'm sorry I ever thought you had.''

''But?'' His grip tightened on her hand. His tormented expression tore at her heart. And yet she knew she had to be sure, absolutely sure, on one last point, before she gave him her answer.

"You aren't moving here just for me, are you? I never meant to...manipulate you into changing for my sake."

"I'm doing everything because I want to, Ari, because it is the right thing for me. I'm hoping it will also be the right thing for us."

And he'd never lied to her. That one truth she did know. More than that, she was now convinced that she could trust this man absolutely.

"It sounds wonderful to me," she whispered.

Clay's relief was almost palpable and his voice was husky with emotion. "So—shall we go get our daughter and tell her we're going to be married?"

Tears of happiness began to overflow as Ariadne nodded.

He started to rise, then went back down on one knee. "I'd like to hear the words, Ari."

"Yes, I'll marry you," she whispered.

"Why?"

"Because I love you."

He kissed the tears away, and held her close. "And I love you, Ariadne."

And that was the whole truth and nothing but.

* * * * *

TRACI ON THE SPOT   BY TRACI

1

Morgan Brigham slowly set down his coffee cup on the kitchen table and stared at the comic strip in the center of his paper. It was nestled in among approximately twenty others that were spread out across two pages. But this was the only one he made a point of reading faithfully each morning at breakfast.

This was the only one that mirrored *her* life.

He read each panel twice, as if he couldn't trust his own eyes. But he could. It was there, in black and white.

Morgan folded the paper slowly, thoughtfully, his mind not on his task. So Traci was getting engaged.

The realization gnawed at the lining of his stomach. He hadn't a clue as to why.

He had even less of a clue why he did what he did next.

Abandoning his coffee, now cool, and the newspaper, and ignoring the fact that this was going to make him late for the office, Morgan went to get a sheet of stationery from the den.

He didn't have much time.

Traci Richardson stared at the last frame she had just drawn. Debating, she glanced at the creature sprawled out on the kitchen floor.

"What do you think, Jeremiah? Too blunt?"

The dog, part bloodhound, part mutt, idly looked up from his rawhide bone at the sound of his name. Jeremiah gave her a look she felt free to interpret as ambivalent.

"Fine help you are. What if Daniel actually reads this and puts two and two together?"

Not that there was all that much chance that the man who had proposed to her, the very prosperous and busy Dr. Daniel Thane, would actually see the comic strip she drew for a living. Not unless the strip was taped to a bicuspid he was examining. Lately Daniel had gotten so busy he'd stopped reading anything but the morning headlines of the *Times*.

Still, you never knew. "I don't want to hurt his feelings," Traci continued, using Jeremiah as a sounding board. "It's just that Traci is overwhelmed by Donald's proposal and, see, she thinks the ring is going to swallow her up." To prove her point, Traci held up the drawing for the dog to view.

This time, he didn't even bother to lift his head.

Traci stared moodily at the small velvet box on the kitchen counter. It had sat there since Daniel had asked her to marry him last Sunday. Even if Daniel never read her comic strip, he was going to suspect something eventually. The very fact that she hadn't grabbed the ring from his hand and slid it onto her finger should have told him that she had doubts about their union.

Traci sighed. Daniel was a catch by any definition. So what was her problem? She kept waiting to be struck by that sunny ray of happiness. Daniel said he wanted to take care of her, to fulfill her every wish.

And he was even willing to let her think about it before she gave him her answer.

Guilt nibbled at her. She should be dancing up and down, not wavering like a weather vane in a gale.

Pronouncing the strip completed, she scribbled her signature in the corner of the last frame and then sighed. Another week's work put to bed. She glanced at the pile of mail on the counter. She'd been bringing it in steadily from the mailbox since Monday, but the stack had gotten no farther than her kitchen. Sorting letters seemed the least heinous of all the annoying chores that faced her.

Traci paused as she noted a long envelope. Morgan Brigham. Why would Morgan be writing to her?

Curious, she tore open the envelope and quickly scanned the short note inside.

Dear Traci,
I'm putting the summerhouse up for sale. Thought you might want to come up and see it one more time before it goes up on the block. Or make a bid for it yourself. If memory serves, you once said you wanted to buy it. Either way, let me know. My number's on the card.

> Take care,
> Morgan

P.S. Got a kick out of *Traci on the Spot* this week.

Traci folded the letter. He read her strip. She hadn't known that. A feeling of pride silently coaxed a smile to her lips. After a beat, though, the rest of his note seeped into her consciousness. He was selling the house.

The summerhouse. A faded white building with brick trim. Suddenly, memories flooded her mind. Long, lazy afternoons that felt as if they would never end.

Morgan.

She looked at the far wall in the family room. There was a large framed photograph of her and Morgan standing before the summerhouse. Traci and Morgan. Morgan and Traci. Back then, it seemed their lives had been permanently intertwined. A bittersweet feeling of loss passed over her.

Traci quickly pulled the telephone over to her on the counter and tapped out the number on the keypad.

* * * * *

*Look for TRACI ON THE SPOT
by Marie Ferrarella, coming to
Silhouette YOURS TRULY
in March 1997.*

Take 4 bestselling love stories FREE

Plus get a FREE surprise gift!

In the tradition of
Anne Rice comes a
daring, darkly sensual
vampire novel by

MAGGIE SHAYNE

BORN IN TWILIGHT

Rendezvous hails bestselling Maggie Shayne's vampire
romance series, WINGS IN THE NIGHT, as
"powerful...riveting...unique...intensely romantic."

Don't miss it, this March, available
wherever Silhouette books are sold.

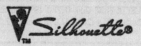

As seen on TV!
Free Gift Offer

With a Free Gift proof-of-purchase from any Silhouette® book,
you can receive a beautiful cubic zirconia pendant.

This gorgeous marquise-shaped stone is a genuine cubic
zirconia—accented by an 18" gold tone necklace.

(Approximate retail value $19.95)

Send for yours today...
compliments of ▼ *Silhouette*®
™

To receive your free gift, a cubic zirconia pendant, send us one original proof-of-purchase, photocopies not accepted, from the back of any Silhouette Romance™, Silhouette Desire®, Silhouette Special Edition®, Silhouette Intimate Moments® or Silhouette Yours Truly™ title available in February, March and April at your favorite retail outlet, together with the Free Gift Certificate, plus a check or money order for $1.65 U.S./$2.15 CAN. (do not send cash) to cover postage and handling, payable to Silhouette Free Gift Offer. We will send you the specified gift. Allow 6 to 8 weeks for delivery. Offer good until April 30, 1997 or while quantities last. Offer valid in the U.S. and Canada only.

Free Gift Certificate

Name: _____

Address: _____

City: _____ State/Province: _____ Zip/Postal Code: _____

Mail this certificate, one proof-of-purchase and a check or money order for postage and handling to: SILHOUETTE FREE GIFT OFFER 1997. In the U.S.: 3010 Walden Avenue, P.O. Box 9077, Buffalo NY 14269-9077. In Canada: P.O. Box 613, Fort Erie, Ontario L2Z 5X3.

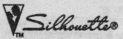

You're About to Become a *Privileged Woman*

Reap the rewards of fabulous free gifts and benefits with proofs-of-purchase from Silhouette and Harlequin books

Pages & Privileges™

It's our way of thanking you for buying our books at your favorite retail stores.

Pages & Privileges™

Harlequin and Silhouette—
the most privileged readers in the world!

For more information about Harlequin and Silhouette's PAGES & PRIVILEGES program call the Pages & Privileges Benefits Desk: 1-503-794-2499

Silhouette®

SSE-PP2